# DEDICATION

This book is dedicated to Carl

MORE BOOKS BY KAREN PASSEY

*Sanctuary For Love*
*When Two World Collide*
*In Your Own Time*

# Contract To Love

Karen Passey

**Contract To Love**

Copyright © 2017 Karen Passey

This book is licensed for your personal enjoyment only. It may not be re-sold or given away to other people.

Karen Passey has asserted her right under the Copyright, Designs and Patents Act 1988 to be identified as the author of this work.

This book is a work of fiction. Names and characters are the product of the author's imagination and any resemblance to actual persons, living or dead, is entirely coincidental.

All rights reserved; no part of this publication may be reproduced or transmitted by any means, electronic, mechanical, photocopying or otherwise, without the prior permission of the publisher. All rights reserved.

Cover design by Lee Ching / Under Cover Designs

Karen Passey

## CHAPTER 1

Sophie swung the car off the road and started up the gravel drive. Turning around the slight bend past the laurel bushes, she was staggered to see a gleaming silver Rolls Royce parked idly outside the cottage door.

Pulling up behind the Rolls, she stopped the engine of her Fiesta and nervously started to walk to the door, fingering the cottage key in her jacket pocket, the crunch of her footsteps appearing to be amplified as she approached nearer the cottage. The door was suddenly flung open unceremoniously.

A tall, expansive male blocked the doorway.

"No interviews!" he burst out aggressively.

"I beg your pardon," Sophie queried, conscious of his penetrating look as he regarded her from head to foot.

"And which of our nation's press do you sustain with titillating gossip, I wonder?" he asked with growling hostility.

"I think that there must be some mistake…" Sophie began.

"The mistake is yours," he replied tartly.

Up until now Sophie had scarcely dared to look fully at him, but she drew herself up to her full five feet six inches, took a deep breath and found the courage to meet his eyes.

A dark, saturnine face with deep, penetrating, brooding eyes held her gaze.

"What are you doing here?" she ventured to ask.

"I think it might be more to the point if *you* explained what *you* are doing here." He was glaring at her, mentally seemingly dissecting her and laying each part of her aside as his eyes traversed her body. Then his eyes shot over her head to the car parked behind his own.

"This is private property. I suggest you explain what you've come for and then clear off," he pronounced tightly.

"I know very well it's private property," Sophie responded hotly, "perhaps you'd tell me what *you* are doing here!"

"I happen to have rented the cottage for six months – which is really none of your damned business. I should prefer it if you would leave immediately. I have work to do."

All Sophie's confidence suddenly drained away as she stared bleakly at him, unable to take in what he had just told her.

"But you can't have…."

"I assure you, young lady, I have paid six months' rent in advance on this Cornish retreat. I needed a place to escape from people like you."

"What do you mean, people like me?" she enquired angrily.

"Well, you're too done up to be borrowing milk at this time of the morning, you have no local accent, you look too smart to have lost your way, so I can only assume that you're some floozy out for a scoop." His eyes swept over her with an aggressive insolence.

"But…she normally never lets it out during the winter," Sophie said feebly, ignoring his accusation, her eyes wandering over the cottage in disbelief.

"If the 'she' you are referring to is Mrs Rayne, then we are not at cross purposes. The very same lady handed me the key in return for rent in advance."

Sophie was too stunned to answer. She flopped onto the stone seat by the cottage door. After all that driving, where was she to go now? If only she had telephoned her mother first, all this wasted journey could have been avoided. Act now, think later! That was Sophie Rayne. Six months! Whatever could her mother have been thinking of? She never went in for long lets normally.

He stepped from the doorway and stood in front of her, legs astride, arms folded. He eyed her with an expression of cool distaste, but when he spoke, his deep voice had a softer edge.

"May I ask who you are?"

"Sophie Rayne. This is my mother's cottage," she replied bleakly.

He towered above her. Six feet three, at least, of solid sinew, dark unruly hair, brown eyes in a deeply attractive face. She felt penned in by his lithe frame, erect in front of her. His tan trousers were belted tightly into a flat, athletic waist, and a fine cream linen shirt covered a broad chest and a pair of extraordinarily wide shoulders. The neck of the shirt was open, exposing the hairs just below his throat. Over his shirt, he wore a carelessly unbuttoned chunky cream woollen jacket with tan suede leather front. In all, she thought, a totally virile male with a very imposing sexuality.

It had been a mistake to sit down. She felt totally

threatened as he stood in this pose, like a predator. She ventured to raise her timid blue eyes to meet his. She'd seen that face before. But where? She studied him, trying to penetrate the depth of her memory, but drew a blank. How could she forget such a superlative male?

He was scowling now, and his normally humorous eyes betrayed an arrogant insolence.

"I trust I pass, Miss Rayne? I do dislike being scrutinised. I am not an object on display. Neither am I an intruder – that is *your* position."

His hostility provoked her, but she apologised, "I'm sorry, you remind me of…of …someone…"

"You remind me of an interloper. If you've quite finished, I have work to do – unless you'd care to do it for me," he added sardonically.

"What sort of work do you do?"

"I'm sure your mother enlightened you," he replied with sarcasm.

"How could she? If I'd known she'd rented out the cottage to you, do you seriously think I would have driven six hours to this sort of situation?"

There was a particular tenseness between them as their eyes met fleetingly.

"Really?" he inclined his head sideways with a nod of total disbelief.

"I didn't drive all night from Manchester just for fun," she said with a note of aggression, which surprised even herself.

"Then why did you come?" he asked coolly, noting her indignation.

"I should have thought that was obvious."

"Do tell me, the obvious often eludes me." His eyes narrowed. "I am so accustomed to looking deeper for the ulterior motive in my line of business."

"It's really of no consequence – not now," she replied perfunctorily, walking towards her car.
He caught her suddenly by the arm and she felt the pressure of his strong grip, even though her jacket.

"Wait!" he commanded.

"What for? It's a long way to drive for insults – and I've had quite enough of those for this week, thank you."

"Ah, ha, so I was right – I sensed a certain dissonance between your body and voice," he said confidently.

"What are you talking about?" she demanded, "and for heaven's sake let go of my arm."

"You've had a stormy row with the boyfriend and come marching down here to think about the damage you've caused," he said, actually tightening the grip on her arm.

"Are you some sort of bully?" she challenged.

"Frequently," he replied, with an enigmatic gleam in his eyes.

"I've arrived to find you here, I'm sorry. Mother never hires out the cottage on such long lets, and certainly never during the winter. I'm really sorry to have bothered you – I'll find somewhere to stay and drive up to London tomorrow."

"Now just a minute, don't be so hasty," he softened, "what sort of a gentleman would I be if I turned the landlady's daughter away?"

"Frankly, I wouldn't have put you in the category of gentleman at all," she said acidly. "Would you please let go of my arm?"
Instead of releasing her, he pulled her further towards him and encircled his arm around her waist. She

stiffened instinctively.

"You arrogant little puss." She felt his warm breath on her cheek. "Put your claws away and try to be civil."

"As I recall, you were being extremely uncivil to me just a moment ago, ordering me to clear off."

"That was before I realised you were the landlady's daughter."

"And please stop referring to me in that way," Sophie said angrily.

"Fair enough," he smiled, "now, you come down of that high horse and let's talk about this sensibly."

"There doesn't seem to be anything to talk about, but if you would kindly release me, it might be a step in the right direction."

"Come inside and let's see what arrangement we can come to." His voice was oddly gentle. "I can hardly let you go off looking for lodgings when the cottage I'm renting is rightfully yours. Besides, there is plenty of room – I'm here on my own."

A quick tremor ran through her.

"But you've paid – in advance," she added sarcastically.

"Touché! Now, will you come inside and have a drink while we discuss what's to be done," he pleaded. He looked steadily at her and she was aware of her lips quivering.

"Thank you," she relented, as he released her and gestured towards the cottage door.

"Take a seat by the fire – here, let me have your coat." His voice was so authoritative as he followed her in.

For Sophie, it felt so strange being invited into her own home.

"Coffee?" he asked as she handed him her jacket.

"Fine, thank you," she said, easing herself into the leather chair by the huge log fire.

Looking around her to the old familiar surroundings, she experienced a strong resentment towards her host. She knew she had no justification to entertain such feelings but his initial attitude towards her had provoked her hostility and she realised that her inclination for men at the moment was at an all-time low, a feeling which had not been brought about simply by Mitch Peters and her sudden flight from Manchester, but a combination of unsavoury incidents and contretemps over the last two or three years. It was no-one's fault but her own, of course. She expected too much from a man.

She had grown up into womanhood cossetted in the cosy warmth of a happy family environment, believing in the honour of man and the decent moral precepts which had been part of her father's code of living. In the last few years she had had some very rude awakenings which had begun to steel her against the unwelcome advances of men with lesser inclination to honour than she had been accustomed to expect. She was not without experience, naturally, and she had not reached twenty-eight without exploring her own sexual possibilities. But she had been disappointed a number of times and had acquired a defensive shield to protect her deeply sensitive emotions.

"Sugar?" the voice from the kitchen called.

"No thank you, I don't," she replied as he walked in carrying a mug of steaming coffee. "Aren't you having any?"

He handed her the mug.

"You have stirred my calm – I shall settle the sea of encroachment on my privacy and restore a steady keel."

"Do you have to be so melodramatic?"

Pouring himself a whisky from the bottle he had removed from the cupboard adjacent to the fireplace, he flopped into the opposite chair. "And do you have to be so impudent, questioning the host?"

His eyes swept over her with an insolence.

Not usually stuck for words, Sophie felt very small and intimidated.

"Now," he said, after a few moments of silence, "how long are you down here for?" There was an air of apparent civility in his manner.

"I don't know – that is, I…"

"A week, a month?" Surely you have some idea?" he asked impatiently.

"Not really, I came on the spur of the moment."

"I thought so," he commented wryly. "Do you usually act so impulsively? You said you have driven from Manchester – you must have been in some hell of a temper if I am any judge!"

"I am not in a temper," she declared tightly, crossing her legs defensively.

"Were – maybe – you're not now, although you are rising fast. Quite a little hot-blood, aren't you?"

"Mr…I'm sorry, I don't know your name – would you please stop…"

"Markham." He hesitated. "Gregory Markham…and would I please stop what?"

So that's it! She knew she'd come across him before. How could she have possibly forgotten that face, that manner, that mood of brooding insolence which she had encountered on the set back in

London. It was some years ago now, though, when she first began work at the TV studio. She had spent the first six months working on a soap opera which had one of the highest audience ratings, and if she recollected correctly, it still had. 'High Rise' – life in a block of flats. She remembered with cringing embarrassment the corny dialogue.

"This dialogue is beginning to sound like your twopenny soap opera," she said savagely.

"Don't knock my work, girl. It keeps bread on the table for a lot of people, and it puts paper in my wallet – and a lot more besides. You ought not to be so disparaging about social necessities. If I didn't write it, someone else would. It serves its purpose and therefore gives me a sense of purpose – which is more than I imagine you feel right now." He emptied his glass with an angry gesture. "Besides, I thought you didn't know me?" he asked cynically. There was a darkness in his eyes, a threat, a smouldering anger which froze her words of protest.

He got up and walked to stand in front of the rear window, apparently staring out. His shoulders were tensed angrily, his legs slightly apart as he flexed the muscles in his buttocks. She found the action sensual and provocative.

"Have you any idea what percentage of our wretched population are forced to live out their miserable lives in infernal tower blocks? They're like the damned pilchards I saw being harvested down in Newlyn last week. "'aul 'em in, squash 'em up, bind 'em together, ha, ha, they'll never get out alive. Squeeze the individuality, dry out the ingenuity, crush all the sensitivity." He suddenly turned and glared at her.

"I'm sure it's not quite as bad as you make out," she tried to protest.

Anger flared in him. "Oh, isn't it? What the devil would *you* know about it?" his nostrils dilated, the muscles in his face tightened. She read the flicker of contempt in his eyes.

"Look …" she began.

"Don't you 'look' me. Have you ever lived in a tower block? What do you know about life, eh?" he asked mockingly. "When have you ever had to grovel and beg? Do you know what it's like living on welfare, ten floors up, three kids, a drunken husband, lousy, rowing neighbours, music blaring from a Blues party three nights a week, watching your life run away in a sewer?"

He was standing in front of her now, blocking out all the light, but his eyes were alive with crazy excitement and his teeth glinted, devilishly white against the rich colour of his face.

She sought to defend herself against his verbal attack and there was a nervous tremor in her voice.

"Mr Markham…I don't think you are being very fair to me…" her voice trailed off in utter confusion. What had provoked this rush of hostile attack? He was clearly incensed. She even suspected he might be slightly drunk. It was as if he had not really been talking to anyone in particular, just sounding off. "You don't have to justify yourself to me," she said dryly in desperation.

"I don't have to justify anything, young lady." The dark flock of hair had fallen across his forehead during his outburst, and he tossed his head angrily.

Sophie sipped her coffee nervously. He's mad, she decided. No-one would ever believe this! He's absolutely mad. I've jumped straight into the fire this time. Mother couldn't possibly have known when she rented the cottage to him. I've met some weird writers in my time, but this one takes the biscuit, she silently considered.

He stood in front of the fire and observed her with a cruel frankness.

"Do you have any idea what I'm talking about?" he asked insolently.

"Oh, I think so," she replied with condescension, "it's simply that you lack the tolerance to listen to anyone else. But feel free, the floor is yours," she said dryly.

His lean and powerful body blocked out all the warmth of the logs blazing behind him. He folded his arms and almost appeared to be pivoting gently on the balls of his feet, his legs slightly apart. It was an extremely sensual movement and she felt sure the he was doing it deliberately, his hips in line with her eyes. She could not fail to observe the emphasis of his body language, and felt slightly disgusted, partly knowing that he was making a deliberate attempt to assert himself physically to intimidate her, and partly because she felt an odd excitement ripple through her just watching him.

"Do you know what worries me?" he asked, not waiting for an answer. "I've created a little monster in 'High Rise' for years now, week after week, thousands of viewers laugh, cry, complain, judge, criticise and even oppose, but they never seem to realise it is only themselves that they are watching."

"You seem to enjoy being on your soap box," Sophie commented dryly, not unaware of her pun.

"I didn't ask for your opinion," he snarled.

"I don't suppose you'd have the patience to listen, anyway," she responded acidly.

He ignored her comment.

"How long do you intend to stay?" he asked curtly.

"I don't intend to stay at all. I shall be away just as soon as I finish my coffee."

"Don't be churlish. I'm trying to be accommodating. If you keep out my way I see no reason why you shouldn't stay. It is your cottage, after all."

"I can imagine the whole village will already be aware that I am here – which is *one* reason I couldn't stay…"

"And another?" he interrupted.

"Did I say there were other reasons?"

"There was an implication in your tone."

"You are too sensitive to my every word. I implied nothing."

"Then you'll stay," he declared emphatically. "Villagers and their gossip are of no consequence. Do you have an overnight bag or just the half-dozen suitcases?" he asked tersely.

"I have some things in the car…" she began.

"Keys!" he demanded, holding out his hand. His whole manner did not brook disobedience. She mutely handed the keys of her car to him and sat staring into the fire.

I must be tired, she rationalised, to respond so willingly to such a manner. I can't possibly stay here, with him, under this roof. There was plenty of room, naturally. The cottage was incorrectly named, since it was really a house. Downstairs it consisted of a large spacious sitting room with a dining area at one end, and a kitchen leading off at the rear. It had originally been two small rooms but her parents had had the adjoining wall removed and the result was much more satisfactory and gave decidedly more light to an otherwise darkened room.

It had been a shambles when they had first bought it nearly twenty years ago – damp, dark, dirty and unlived-in for years before that. Over the years they had spent a great deal of money renovating the place, spending much of their holidays working to improve it. A damp course had been one of the first jobs, and a new roof, along with replacement floors. There had been no electricity or running water, and for a long time, while they made the cottage habitable, their holidays had been spent in a small caravan, parked in the huge gardens and land which surrounded the property.

Looking at the solid grey, Cornish stone walls, she remembered that summer when she was nine years old and helped to 'do her bit' as her mother had put it. She had chipped and chipped away at the unnecessary plaster on the walls and at the end of each day had been covered from head to foot in plaster dust, and looked rather like one of the children in an old photograph she had of Cornish children at the turn of the century, working in the St Austell clay pits.

The ancient fireplace with seats set back in the wall either side had been retained and her mother had made attractive cushions to lay inside the seats for added comfort and warmth. The cottage boasted original oak beams and great care had been taken to retain the character of the place. Any additions that were made had been totally in keeping with the style of the cottage. The old staircase leading off had been torn out. It was riddled with woodworm and dry rot and only constituted a danger anyway. It had been carefully replaced with a spiral stairway made of oak. Created and polished, it was a work of art – built, naturally enough, by a local man.

Years ago, according to the deeds, the cottage had belonged to a farm labourer, who had seen no use for a bathroom, so an extension had been built at the side of the kitchen – in matching stone, naturally. It was not possible structurally to accommodate a bathroom up the stairs. There were four small, but adequate bedrooms, one with a view across the cliffs to the Atlantic on a clear day. It was only a mile from the coast, but the mists could float in from that same Atlantic and envelop the whole area in a dull, grey cloud, at any time. The same mists brought the dampness and at times the very walls seemed to perspire, leaving a salty deposit from the aged stone.

Without detracting from the 'olde-worlde' charm of the place, her parents had had one or two modern innovations made at the cottage. An immersion heater, carefully concealed in a wall cavity, now a cupboard, that also served as an 'airing space', ensured plenty of hot water. Wall lighting in the bedrooms was so contrived to give just the right effect in the small, low, oak-beamed-ceiling rooms. The whole cottage had a surfeit of tiny wall cupboards and recesses and nooks and crannies that had excited her imagination as a child.

Her car started outside and she jumped up to see Gregory Markham moving the vehicle to around the side of the cottage, out of view of anyone coming to the front door. A few minutes later he appeared carrying her two suitcases.

"Your car stinks! Have you had fish in it at some time?"

"Oh!" she shrieked, "I quite forgot, I bought some fish in Newlyn earlier on. Finding you here, it completely went from my mind…"

"From the smell of it you've brought the boatload with you," he replied peremptorily, dropping the cases and going back outside to the car.
When he reappeared, he was carrying a cardboard box of groceries and the fish placed on top.

"What is it?" he asked, opening the paper. "Ah! Hake. Now, what I wouldn't give to a good woman who knows how to do justice to a decent piece of hake," he smirked, licking his lips as he went into the kitchen.

"Huh!" she snorted ungraciously, following him. "Good heavens! Don't you ever wash up?" she exploded. A mountain of dirty crockery and empty tins and packets of all descriptions faced her.

"Sometimes," he laughed at her expression, "when I'm having company – but you arrived somewhat unexpectedly and have caught me out!"
She slammed the kitchen door in his face and heard him climb up the stairs, still laughing, a deep, mocking laugh.

She was indignant. The cottage kitchen in this state! It was more than any self-respecting woman could stand. Rolling up her sleeves of her sweater she set about making some order out of the mêlée which confronted her. Out of the frying pan, into the fire, Sophie, she thought, squeezing the green liquid into the hot water and watching the bubbles rise. What on earth have I driven myself into? And what on earth could she tell her mother? Mother, with all her puritan ideals – what would she make out of this little situation?

Well, clearly the idea of spending a few weeks gathering herself together would be out of the question. She knew she should never have come.

If she were not such a creature of impulse she would never have been in this situation now, she realised. She had always managed to jump into everything with two feet, then find she was out of her depth. That was how she managed to be so involved with Mitch Peters in the first place. If only she had the sense to realise how easily she was slipping into involvement with him, it might have been possible to extricate herself sooner and have avoided all the hurt and frustration.

She should have realised from the start that he was just the sort of man who would try to have his own way, at any cost, with anyone and she was only just another woman to him.

Well, this time, Sophie Rayne, she silently observed, your stupidity and impulsiveness have probably cost you your job. That small thought had not really crossed her mind up to now. For the last few hours she had been totally obsessed with the fact that she had very nearly lost her reputation and self-respect. Mitch Peters was not a man to give a jot about either of those things.

In fact, he had seemed hell-bent on taking both from her. Yes, the job was secondary to her. She would be able to find another job quite easily in London. She had not made contacts in the business over the last five years for nothing. She had earned the respect of any producer she had ever worked with and never left any post without regret on both sides. Not until now, anyway. It crossed her mind that Mitch might try to stop her getting another job but she reassured herself with the fact that her past track record would be enough to convince the moguls of her true value. It would be obvious to anyone, she reasoned, that any character assassination undertaken by Mitch Peters would be vindictive and spurious.

Later on, she would telephone Lionel in Staff Relations and explain everything – well, nearly everything!

Naturally, she'd have to be careful how she related the situation, but she felt confident he would understand her predicament and the reason for her rapid departure from a job! Her one objective had been to get out of Manchester as quickly as possible, and rushing back to her hotel, she had packed all her things and driven straight towards Birmingham, where she had stopped for coffee and a snack near the Television Studios in the city centre. She realised too late now how foolish she had been, when an old colleague, Kirsty Gerrard, whom she had never really liked, noticed her alone at the corner table and made a great show of joining her.

It had been difficult to get rid of Kirsty, whose prying nature and eagerness to dwell on others' miseries was enough to cause a lot of people to want to shake off her company at midnight. She had worked with Kirsty on a production in London, just about the time she had first encountered Mitch Peters. In fact, Sophie later found out that Kirsty had been Mitch's 'companion' at that time. When Sophie had moved up to the Manchester studios to work on a two-month contract, she was unaware that Mitch

Peters had been responsible for asking for her to be his Research Assistant but at the last minute he was unable to make the documentary. It had been assigned to another producer, who insisted that Sophie would still be his choice for the job, especially since her special knowledge of economic and social conditions of the Manchester area was second to none!

"Darling, I thought you were working in Manchester with Mitch?" Kirsty's opening remarks had been.

Sophie could almost sense Kirsty's information-seeking tentacles lacing themselves around with eager curiosity. Of course, most people in the business knew that a year after that first documentary which she had eventually done with Brad Merrill, a follow-up programme had been sought and she had been automatic choice for Research Assistant. Brad had been filming in America when Mitch had been given this second programme. From Sophie's point of view, it had been a traumatic experience working with Mitch. He was a fiery, domineering, erratic man.

He had none of Brad's calm, positive approach that encouraged responses from colleagues. No, Mitch was something quite different. He was attractive, in a rugged sort of way and he had a swagger that seemed to carry him forward, physically and metaphorically. He never disguised the fact that he liked women and he made no secret of recounting his exploits. In most cases, what he revealed was true, but if his escapade with a woman had not come up to his expectations, his art as a narrator never failed him, and many an innocent female had unknowingly been an accessory to his libidinous activities.

"I thought that contract didn't finish for another week?" Kirsty persisted.

"There's just the editing now, we were ahead of the schedule."

"And what are you working on?" Sophie asked after a pause, carefully avoiding answering what Kirsty really wanted to know.

"Nothing too special. How's Mitch?" she held Sophie's eyes mercilessly, predator-like in her anxiety for news of her former lover.

"I thought you weren't bothered with him these days?" Sophie evaded.

"Is he still in Manchester?"

"Why, yes," Sophie had tried to sound non-committal.

"But if the contract is finished, why isn't he with you then?" Kirsty never gave up. A lot of people said she was just too vapid and her dogged questioning was all quite innocent and childlike, but Sophie preferred to think that Kirsty was simply bad-mannered, ignorant and totally lacking in tact, all of which had very little to do with innocence.

Just how much Kirsty knew, Sophie was not sure. "Have you been in touch with him lately?" she asked.

"You know he has nothing to do with me now," Kirsty pouted. "That's why he wanted you last year to do the original documentary. He got his way in the end, though, didn't he?"

"I wouldn't say that," she replied, smiling inwardly.

"That's not what I heard," Kirsty rejoined.

Sophie stiffened instinctively. Obviously, Mitch had lost no time in propagating his fertile seeds of invention. But she didn't intend to elaborate to someone like Kirsty who was an empty-headed young lady, really, too full of other peoples' activities to have any serious machinations of her own. It was no surprise the she only held her job with the company because her father was in the business. She was usually diverted to where she could do least damage as far as the job was concerned.

"Are you on your way home, then?" Kirsty asked.

"Yes," Sophie lied, knowing that if Mitch did contact Kirsty it would be better if he was misled.

"You're not driving down to London tonight, are you?"

"I must drive on tonight," Sophie insisted, gulping her last mouthful of coffee. "I have lots of things to attend to in the morning. Besides, what is there to stay in Birmingham for?"

"You can share my room at the hotel, if you like."

The thought was more than Sophie could bear.

"Lovely of you to offer, Kirsty, but I thought I'd take advantage of the empty roads, thanks all the same."

She could quite easily have stayed in Manchester, Birmingham, Oxford or London, but it had been in her mind to get down to Cornwall. There, she would feel free and cleansed.

By the time she had reached Penzance, all her anger and frustration had been driven from her. Four hours of driving through the night from Birmingham had given Sophie plenty of time to reflect and in the coldness of the early morning she thought she had made the right decision. She had reasoned with herself along the motorway, street and lane, and through the network of her mind had coursed a myriad thoughts. It was as if the car had instinctively taken her to her destination whilst her brain was occupied in retrospection, recrimination and resolution.

Now she was not so sure she had made the right decision at all. The door opened onto her thoughts and the kitchen.

"Not finished?" he taunted. "You were so long I was convinced you were preparing an early lunch."

She wiped her hands on the towel, ignoring his comment, and made to leave the kitchen. He blocked the doorway.

"Very impressive!" he beamed, looking over her shoulder.

"I'm sure you could achieve the same result if you tried once in a while," she replied caustically.

"Without a doubt, but women are better in the kitchen. However, we manage when necessary. Fortunately, men have an inherent capacity to cope without the fair sex. Women stifle a man, strangle his motives, discipline his life, and cultivate a 'yes' man for their own unscrupulous ends. In short they destroy a man."

"No doubt your embittered attitude reflects in your writing. Personally, I never watch your melodramas," she said scathingly.

"I did not suppose for one moment that you would," he said moving back into the room. "Needless to say, I imagine that you are only familiar with my soap opera. I do write more sophisticated works, but naturally, I rarely use the name Markham.

I found a long time ago that it was wise to have my more serious writings under an assumed name. It's less in demand of course, but then serious comment usually is. As you may realise, most of the population want their thinking done for them. Television has been partly responsible for perpetrating its own evils, of course. It's my belief that we have brainwashed the populace into switching on the 'box' in order to 'switch on' – if you get my meaning."

"Very profound!" she said softly from the leather chair beside the fire.

"Not really – it's rather obvious if you know people. I never quite know which I despise more, the apathy of the public or the celluloid people who perpetrate the corruption."

"And where do you come in? Your contribution is in actually producing the trash," she replied, mentally making a note that he had used her father's phrase about the 'celluloid' people of TV.

He was stretched in the other fireside chair, his lounging air a pose. He jumped up excitedly and wagged his finger accusingly at her.

"That's got nothing to do with it. If a market is there, someone will fill the gap. Besides, it depends on which of my work you refer to. If you are talking about 'High Rise', then I have underestimated your intelligence." He glared at her.

"On the contrary, you made quite a scathing comment about the soap opera yourself."

"You misunderstood it, I think. The programme is a very necessary social comment. My regret is that those to whom it is directed are unaware of its relevance." There was a sigh of intolerance in his voice as he flung himself bodily into the chair. "They see it simply as a series of stories, changing from week to week. They become involved, 'participate in it' is the expression the Mickey Mouse Mob call it, but I maintain they fail to connect the message that is peddled."

"But if that happened you might find yourself out of work," Sophie replied.

"Therein lies my confidence," he said, pulling himself up in the chair and crossing his legs with an exaggerated movement. "My ability to interpret the whims of people assures me of an extremely satisfactory employment until such time as I decide to pull out the plug and say, 'No more of this - your dreary domestic drama has plagued me for long enough'." He inclined his head dramatically and gestured with a wide sweep of his arm, just as if he were giving a performance himself.

"So you agree, it is a dreary, domestic drama?" she picked up his statement quickly.

"Not at all," he asserted arrogantly, "I just allow myself the privilege of disagreeing or agreeing as I see fit."

"Rather an arbitrary attitude to hold, if I might say so."

There was a cynical twist of the lips, an excuse for a smile, perhaps, as he said savagely, "Never try to defeat me with words – I have more at my command than you do. I've been around longer!"

Their eyes met and the fiery anger in his expression placed her beneath contempt.

"I despise a woman who must have the last word," he added, "however adroit she may be with her vocabulary."

"My impression is that you simply despise

women!" Sophie responded quickly.

"How little you know!" he mocked. "However, I am quite willing to demonstrate my deference to the fair sex by preparing lunch. Perhaps you'd not object to sharing your piece of fish with a humble writer?" He wrung his hands dramatically, cringing like the Uriah Heep of Dickens' novel, inclining his head to one side, whining with the obsequious tone of the importuning Mr Heep.

She was amused and surprised by his sudden change of attitude.

"This I must see," she agreed, starting up the spiral stair.

"I've removed your suitcases to the bedroom," he called after her.

Relief at reaching the bedroom was quickly changed to shock. Her room, the one she always used, was an improvised study for Mr Markham. Her orderly mind was quite offended by the disorganised mess she walked into. The bed was pushed against the wall, an old typewriter was balanced on the table under the window amid a pile of papers and books. The floor was littered with more books, notes, screwed up balls of paper, and to her ultimate disgust, an empty whisky bottle.

She was about to close the door discreetly but her eyes rested on a photograph balanced precariously amongst the piles of books. Feminine curiosity got the better of her, and she picked up the frame.

"My family," a voice boomed behind her. Sophie coloured uncomfortably and attempted an apology.

"Your room is the next one!" He snatched the photograph from her and she fled out.

## CHAPTER 2

Sophie had realised that Gregory Markham must have been married, but she was more than curious as to why he should secrete himself in her mother's cottage and where his wife and two children fitted into the scheme of things. It was none of her business, of course, but she could not help wondering as she lay on the bed, fully-clothed, to relax before the lunch he had promised. As all the possible stories raced through her mind, she began to drift into a drowsy sleep.

A sharp rap at the bedroom door about an hour later brought her quickly to her senses.

"If you would care to grace our table, Miss Rayne, a hasty, but tasty lunch has been prepared for mutual benefit," Markham called and promptly thumped back down the staircase.

He had watched her all the way down the stairs. Slouched lazily in the fireside chair, a half empty glass in his hand, there was a glazed look in his eyes as he studied every detail, his face quite expressionless. He pulled himself up from the chair, brought his glass to the table and gestured perfunctorily for her to serve out the meal.

She said nothing.

He ate without a single word of comment.

The delicious hake mousse and green salad he had prepared was soon eaten in the pregnant silence. When she caught his eye, the steady, enigmatic half-smile was unchanging. He had signalled nonchalantly with one finger for her to clear away and then had disappeared upstairs as she cleared away the lunch things and washed up, and she imagined he was sleeping off the effects of the contents of his glass.

That was something she could never understand. How does a perfectly intelligent being allow himself to succumb to the degradation of alcohol, to wallow in that brain-numbing state where the sharp edges of reality are smoothed and sounds are softened, decisions are easy to make and thoughts are mollified as life appears to mellow? The thought disgusted her. It reminded her immediately of the debasing scene she had endured with Mitch Peters and how she had come to be so embarrassingly entangled with him on that Saturday evening.

From the start, he had duped her into believing she was able to trust him. Somehow, he had managed to convince her that he was only after mental stimulation with her. She had only herself to blame. She had warded off the advances of worse wolves than Mitch Peters in the past and it was so unlike her not to be more perceptive. In four weeks, he had not made a single pass at her and he had gone out of his way to be affable but distant. He had anticipated her admirably. It had been a carefully calculated plot to seduce her and she had almost fallen for it.

In the fifth week, when taking final film footage of the nineteenth century slums, he relapsed into a melancholy frame she had never experienced with him before.

"I were born in Ancoats, you know."

"Really?" she asked, interest flashing into her eyes, "where exactly, I've made quite a study of Manchester?"

"One o' them side streets off the Old'am Road, lass," he smiled, lapsing into the vernacular.

Foolishly she had warmed to him, forgiving all the scurrilous gossip and tales of sexual encounters. He had found her Achilles heel. Her love of the past, especially social history, had been her undoing. He invited her out to dinner that night, then took her back to the bar at the studios in Water Street.

"Brought a touch o' class in with you tonight, Mitch lad, the bartender remarked.

Sophie had ignored the comment and been oblivious to the knowing glances and winks of some of the company present. They had sat apart from everyone, Mitch as garrulous as ever, but surprisingly interesting, never broaching on the intimate, discussing the documentary, what to do next, and so on. She found herself liking him, almost, seeing another side to Mitch Peters. He was respectful and interested in her, but kept himself in total check the whole evening. It must have nearly killed him, she reflected later. Walking her back to the hotel he stopped in Deansgate, pulled her towards him, tilted her chin and looked intently at her.

"You're a grand lass, Sophie, I've enjoyed meself, tonight at least. I 'ate Manchester. I were born 'ere and the bit I were born in I damned near killed meself to get out of. Me mam died in Chethams 'ospital, me dad cleared off six weeks later wi' a singer from Gates'ead. I've two brothers and a sister somewhere – we lost touch years ago." He kissed her lightly on the cheek. 'Appen you'll 'ave dinner wi' me again sometime, eh, lass?"

"You're so different, talking in your native accent. I've enjoyed the evening so much," she said guilelessly. "Yes, I'd love to."

That was just the beginning. For the rest of that week he behaved without the slightest impropriety. Little did she realise he was preparing to move in for the kill. On the Saturday night he arrived, slightly worse for drink, apologising of course. He'd had some rather bad news and had one glass too many, he explained.

Sophie felt he'd had one bottle too many.

She had not finished dressing, but she had had to let him into her room because he was making such a scene outside in the corridor and the people from the next room had made an obvious appearance at their door. Mitch lay on the bed and started rambling on about all his troubles catching up with him. Foolishly, she felt sorry for him. She sat by him on the edge of the bed. He was quiet for a moment, then he reached out for her hand.

"You're a decent girl, Sophie. You make a fellow feel good. When I'm with you, I …" his voice trailed off.

"You what?" she enquired a second or two later.

"You'd never believe me."

"Try me," she said guilelessly.

"Lie down by me," he patted the bed.

She knew she had made a terrible mistake. Within seconds he started to tear at her blouse and his heavy hands began pawing at her like a crazy, incensed creature. He rolled over on top of her, bearing down heavily, his breath reeking of the whisky he had been soaking up before he had arrived.

"You're a hard creature to tame, Sophie Rayne. But I'm going to win that bet if it's the last thing I do."

"What bet?" she shrieked.

"Come on, pet, don't play the innocent with me. You know damned well I never lose on a woman."

Her face a haunted white, she stared up at him, feeling his incensed breath scorching her cheeks.

"You *are* a louse, after all," she flared.

He caught aggressively at her thinly-clad shoulders, his fat fingers pressing the bone painfully.

"Just relax, Sophie, you might enjoy it wi' an Ancoats lad, we're a breed apart, dost tha' not know that, lass?" he jeered in his native accent. "I really thought tha' liked me wi' a touch o' me Mancunian roughness."

Whilst he was fumbling to undo his trousers with one hand and balancing with the other, she caught him unawares, gave a mighty heave against his weighty body and he toppled straight off the edge of the bed. She rushed to the door, flung it open and ran along the corridor to the room of one of the cameramen, banged anxiously on his door and threw herself into his arms when he opened up to such frantic knocking.

The sickening memory of that night forced her to think of what she should do now. Racing off into the night was one thing. Finding yourself jumping from the frying pan into the fire was another. She had walked out on a job only days before it was due to finish.

Now she had to face Lionel or at least talk to him on the 'phone and make her explanations. That would be the first step. Where she would go from there remained to be seen. Her plan had been to stay at the cottage for a while, but with that possibility closed to her, she would have to return to London. And if she was in London then she might just as well be at work. With this thought in mind she determined to contact Lionel and make the necessary arrangements and return to London that afternoon.

The sound of the typewriter from the room above her jolted Sophie into action and she crept out of the front door and made her way to the 'phone box at the far end of the village. She had wanted to arouse as little notice as possible and took the back path behind the cottage, skirting the fields, taking herself quite out of her way to start with. Had she walked straight through the village, no doubt the village gossip, Mrs Tregarn, would be peering from her store window and the news would be flashed to every member of the community.

Mrs Tregarn was an ample woman in every respect. She was of average height, powerfully-built with huge hams of fleshy arms. Her features were distinctive and gross, her head large and her lips fleshy. She had a large Roman nose, dark, piercing, impudent eyes and a profusion of grey hair, drawn untidily on top of her head into a 'bun'.

Her face had the ruddy look of a farmworker who has seen too much sun and she gave the impression of being perpetually flustered, breathless and constantly brushed wisps of stray hair from her face. Like the store she owned, she always exuded an odour of mustiness and camphor balls.

For all that, Sophie liked her for her genuine warmth and her hospitality, but she had no particular wish to encounter her this afternoon.

No-one driving through the village would realise that there was a telephone box. It was tucked away behind the trees, down the side of a derelict old building along a very narrow part of the road.

It was as if the Cornish had a distrust of the instrument, secreted behind the trees, the lamp in the box inevitably never working, and, Sophie felt, no-one seemed to have been in the 'phone box from one year to the next, for the same old debris on the floor and the spiders and webs welcomed her whenever she had to use the 'phone.

Unwelcoming though the telephone box was, she was grateful to reach its sanctuary. A biting, cold wind had risen and was stinging her face with its sharpness. She carefully assembled her pile of coins in readiness for a long conversation with Lionel and began dialling London.

There was a sharp rap on the window.

Sophie jumped, startled to see Willy Hoskins, the village postboy, grinning at her through the window.

"'E's not workin', m'dear," he shouted.

Sophie put down the 'phone and attempted to get a dialling tone.

He was right, of course. That would account for his self-satisfied grin.

"You furriners is always gettin' on that damned thing," Willy said as she gathered her coins and left the box.

"How long has it been out of order, Willy?"

"I'm not sure, m'dear. That big toff up at your cottage, 'e 'ad trouble last week. Why don't 'e come in the Office an' do your talkin' on Miss Trevose's instrument? 'Er won't mind a bit. That writer chap, 'e did, spoke to people in London 'e did, too, sure enough."

"How did you know he's a writer?"

"Everybody knows that, Miss Sophie. Mrs Tregarn, now she's seen 'im on the television too. ''E's quite famous, ain't 'e? Mrs Tregarn took 'im 'is provisions round from 'er store, she did, too. She's spoke to 'im more'n once, I declare. Well, 'e's a famous person 'e is, isn't that so, Miss Sophie?"

"Yes, I do believe so," she replied offhandedly, starting to walk away from him.

"'Ere, ain't you comin' to th'Office, like I suggested?" Willy seemed affronted.

"No, it's not that important, Willy, thanks all the same."

And doubtless her business would be broadcast across the whole of West Penwith if she did call at the Post Office and trouble Miss Trevose.

"Are you stayin' ere long, Miss Sophie?" Willy called after her.

Rather than commit herself one way or the other, she pretended his voice was lost in the wind and did not bother to reply. No sense in trying to hide the fact that she was in the village now! And no doubt all manner of stories would be fabricated alluding to a variety of 'illicit goin's on' at that Mrs Rayne's cottage. She strode crossly back to the cottage, waving briefly to Mrs Tregarn as she passed the store, and marched up the gravel path to find Gregory Markham standing at the front door.

Where the hell have you been?" he demanded furiously.

"It's none of your business. Do you think you're my keeper or something?" She was already angry and his appearance had only served to increase her impatience. From start to finish, things had gone completely wrong, and when that happened, Sophie's temper began to fray.

"You might at least let a body know when you're going out. I was banging on the floor like a fool, for you to come upstairs."

"Oh, were you now, well I happened to have business of my own to attend to. I didn't drive down here to wait on you!"

"No doubt you have just found that the telephone is out of order?" his voice changed unexpectedly and there was a hint of a smile in his face.

Sophie felt foolish. He seemed to have the ability to read her like a book. She declined to reply and went to brush past him in the doorway.

He grabbed her fiercely and she stiffened instinctively. The exciting smell of his aftershave tingled her nostrils as he brought his face close to hers and smiled at her, more amused than disconcerted by her rudeness.

"Take a hold of your exasperation. The world is not scheming against *you* in particular. That 'phone has been out of order since Christmas. I reported it last week again, but you know how the Cornish move. Why not use the Post Office 'phone?"

"I don't want my life broadcast across West Penwith. What I have to say I don't particularly want overheard by the postmistress to be related at length at the whist drive on a Friday night in the Village Institute. I have some explaining to do that calls for some small measure of privacy. I'll telephone on my way through Penzance. Now, will you please let go of me?" She attempted to pull herself free of him, expecting a battle, like the previous occasion when she had arrived earlier on that morning, but he let her go immediately and stepped aside for her to pass into the cottage. He followed quickly on her heels, went straight into the kitchen and called to her as she was climbing the stairs.

"I'll make you a coffee, you'll feel better."
Her murmured thanks were lost to him as he began whistling cheerfully in the kitchen. Minutes later he appeared in her bedroom.

"Here," he said, handing her a mug of coffee and sitting, legs straddled out in front of him in the small chair behind the door.

"Now, I suggest you drive *into*, not through, Penzance, make your 'phone call, then come back here. You're pretty chewed up about something. The best thing to do in such circumstances is to pause and quietly reflect. I imagine you need a decent night's sleep and the whole situation will take on a different perspective tomorrow, I promise you." His voice was slow, deliberate and mellow, and Sophie found herself relaxing under the almost hypnotic tone. "Believe me," he continued, "I've been there too! I've learned the best remedies!" He gave her a beguiling smile.

"You have my car keys," she responded.

"So I do," he agreed, taking them from his trouser pocket and handing them to her. "Are you a safe driver?" he asked her jokingly.

"I like to think so," she replied imperturbably.

"In that case, I shall join you on the jaunt to Penzance. I have a call to make myself and will avail myself of your sober drive!" He disappeared from the room before she could reply.

This must be quite a come-down for you," Sophie attempted at a conversation. He had been silent most of the six miles into Penzance and the quiet had given her time to compose herself.

"Not at all, I only drive the Rolls for long journeys as a rule. Comfort is of the essence. When I'm up in town I quite frequently use a taxi – or Robin's small runabout.

"Who is Robin?" she enquired, fancying it to be the nickname of the very attractive woman in the photograph back at the cottage.

"My son. I bought him a small car for his birthday." His voice was cold.

"I'm surprised you have a son that age. You scarcely look old enough." Her voice was genuinely flattering.

He eased round in the seat as if to search her face, and finding the sincerity not wanting, he smiled at her warmly.

"You must remember, my dear girl, I was a hungry man when I left University. Delving in the archives in search of our noble forebears for three years had filled me with concupiscence. I started early!"
She was embarrassed by the frankness of his reply.

"But the photograph – the children – they look very young," she said, reddening.

"I like to remember them all as they were then, not now. Things have changed – memories haven't though!" His voice was spiritless and empty. It was obviously the end of the conversation. Nothing else was said as she parked in the main car park, agreeing to meet him within the hour.

"Why the hell didn't you ring me? I could have sorted Mitch Peters out!" Lionel Fairfax shouted down the telephone line from London.

Sophie was totally taken aback. No doubt the whole story had reached Lionel's ears from Mitch. The wrong story! His side of it, of course!

"As it is, it will take some smoothing out now – despite the strength of your reputation," Lionel continued, not allowing Sophie a word in the conversation, "you're supposed to be able to handle situations like that – it's explosive, I know, but we can't let emotions rule our job!"

Emotions! Was that all Lionel could see in this situation?

She had gone over the whole episode so many times on the drive to Penzance, as if by rinsing it so often she could endeavour to clear the stains from her mind. Her whole reputation had been impugned. Later, when Bill, the cameraman, assured her that Mitch had left the room, she had gone back and locked herself in for the rest of the night.

She heard nothing from Mitch and presented herself at the studios on Monday as if the episode had never taken place. She had underestimated Mitch, however. He had spent much of his time since Saturday convincing his cronies that he had seduced the 'high and mighty' Sophie Rayne and rumours of her lack of frigidity were being banded around the studio. Those who had urged him on had paid their debt in full. Fifty pounds!

She never knew how she would live down the ignominy of that awful situation. All she could do was rely on Bill to make sure the truth was told. It was difficult, but for the next two days she kept herself aloof from the comments and knowing glances. It would have been too undignified to involve herself in explanations. Silence is the best answer to the fool!

On the Tuesday night, they had finished filming very late and she had been attending to some paperwork in the studio office they had been assigned for the duration of the contract. Mitch had come into the office and caused an argument over the Schedule Sheets for the following final day's shooting. He attempted to find any flaw he could in her work. He resented being ignored by her, which is precisely what she had done in the last two days. He goaded her about her intellectual abilities and finally insulted her sexuality – or lack of it.

Sophie, though impulsive, had quietly proceeded to pack up her work for the evening, leaving everything neat and tidy, as usual, for the next day. She said not a word to him until she reached for her jacket just as Bill came in to take her to the hotel, as previously arranged. She was grateful for a witness.

"Mitch, in five years in television I have never once had my work questioned. If I had, I should have been grateful, for the guiding hand of experience. I can take advice, but I will *not* tolerate insult. But it is not for that that I leave this job tonight. I am simply not prepared to listen to the fatuous remarks and lies about my private life. I also suggest that you return the money to your colleagues – you took it from them under false pretences. Incidentally, to get that close to me would cost a lot more than fifty pounds!"
Mitch Peters was speechless.

"And by the way, I shall be contacting the studio director in London. I am not intending to return to work with you tomorrow – or ever again."

A tremulous anger in her voice, she tossed her head contemptuously and left with Bill.

At first, she was just too stunned to reply to Lionel's invective. She felt how unjust and one-sided it had all been. Despite her tremendous respect for Lionel, she felt as if she was on the carpet, being 'put down' gently and politely. Men always seemed to come out of situations like this better than their female counterparts, she reflected. It was as if they sided with each other at times like this – a private club – "don't let the women in, this is an exclusive enclave. We are permitted all manner of liberties, but not women. Oh, no! We can't have them thinking that they have equality in this!"

Thomas Hardy's double standard again. Even at school, she had felt resentful where the painful message of double standard had been brought home to her in 'Tess of the D'Urbervilles'. It was alright for a man to err, but a woman, oh no! There would be no accepting that. She realised that in this case, she had not erred, but she had dared to let her emotions take over whilst on a contract. Perhaps she was over-reacting. After all, Lionel did say he'd fix up something for her in three or four weeks. Maybe he was simply trying to make a point and assert his authority and position.

"You've ruffled a few feathers," he had said, when she tried to put her side of the situation. "You simply can't walk out on a job, Sophie, darling. Why not take some of the holiday you are owed. Let things settle down for a while. I can't promise anything at the present, but I definitely will be able to come up with something in a few weeks. The whole thing will have blown over by then and I shall be able to broach your name with confidence."

Sophie thanked him sarcastically for his trouble and put down the 'phone in a raging fury.

She had expected some sort of co-operation from Lionel Fairfax. He was Head of Staff Relations, but at least he had some inkling of her character and this was not a teacup of her own brewing. With that 'l'esprit d'escalier' as she stomped back to her car, she wished she had told him to keep his job. She was raging with the injustice of her treatment and the only consolation was that she could expect to be on full pay and take the polite leave of absence as legitimate holiday which was owed to her.

With an angry scowl spoiling her face, she slammed the car door and sat to wait for Gregory Markham's return.

## CHAPTER 3

It was quite out of character for Sophie to discuss her private affairs with anyone, let alone a virtual stranger. But somehow it seemed different with Gregory Markham. He had an ineffable way of drawing information out of her. By the time they reached the cottage, Sophie had revealed her dilemma to him. She had expected him to break out into paroxysms of laughter over her subjugation of the philandering Mitch Peters, but he was very sensitive to her feelings.

It was only later, sitting beside the fire, that she began to wonder if she had done the right thing in baring her soul to him. She also regretted having agreed to stay at the cottage that night.

Sometime during the journey back from Penzance she had acquiesced, but not without some coaxing on his part, and it was now that she began to be suspicious of his motives.

"Would you like a glass of mulled wine?" He broke in her thoughts.

"Do you have some?" she asked stupidly.

"Not immediately, but I can soon muster it together for you, it's just the job on a cold afternoon. I've all the ingredients," he said, rising and going to the cupboard at the side of the fireplace. "Cinnamon, lemon, sugar and of course," he smiled, producing a large bottle of red wine from the cupboard, "the essential ingredient."

"I'd love it," she responded, remembering the warm glow she had experienced years earlier. Half a dozen of her colleagues at Oxford had called to her rooms unexpectedly on her birthday, one cold, December morning, and initiated her into the delectable delights of spicy, mulled wine.

"You appear to be in a vacuum," Gregory stood in front of her, holding a large glass of mulled wine.

"That was quick," she commented, taking it from him.

"Not really, you've been daydreaming for the last half-an-hour or so, didn't you realise?"

"I'm so sorry, was I really? Actually, I was just – does that sort of thing happen to you?"

"What sort of thing?"

"Mind-wandering," she said vaguely.

"Frequently. Especially when I've been drinking!" he laughed.

"I'm not talking about the vagaries of being drunk or fuddled. Mm!" she sipped the wine and a ripple of sheer pleasure went through her.

"Then what are you talking about?"

"You know, when someone says something to you or … it might be just a sensation, a smell, a touch, a sound … and your mind races immediately through a myriad passages of the imagination to another time, another place, another person, another feeling, and that in turn sets off a whole chain of thoughts – half-forgotten things, people, scenes, actions, words – it's rather like living parts of your life over again, but with the added advantage of maturity and the secret comfort of retrospection."

"And is that what happened to you just now?" he asked, intrigued.

"It happens all the time. I always seem to be looking back."

"Maybe looking back offers more comfort than looking forward."

"Oh, I doubt if it's a conscious action. What I mean is …" she looked at him seated in the fireside chair opposite, searching his face for sincerity and found it not wanting.

"Yes, go on …"

"I don't do it deliberately. I find I can't help myself. But it happens all the time. I'm not making myself very clear, am I?"

"Perfectly. It's indicative of a very quick brain," he assured her, "association of ideas, hyperactive mind. It could be you're not getting enough stimulation."

She tensed, sensing he was laughing at her.

"Not that kind of stimulation," he grinned, realising immediately the effect of his words.

"I'm sorry, I'm naturally on my guard."

"Why? Why be on your guard all the time? Let yourself go. If someone is having a quiet laugh at you sometime, respond to it with that quick, intelligent brain of yours. Don't shrivel up and cut the emotions dead! One cutting remark earns another."

"I tried that earlier on with you – it led to …"

"It led to nothing," he interrupted sharply, "I simply told you that I despise a woman who must have the last word."

"Exactly!" she replied smugly.

"Not at all, you simply chose the wrong

adversary at the wrong time of the day!"

"I doubt if there would ever be a right time of the day with you," came her reply.

"Oh, I don't know so much," his voice was suggestive, "we shall have to wait and see. More wine?" he changed the subject.

"Please. I don't normally drink very much, but there is something about mulled wine that reminds me … see, there I go again, remembering, always going back, reflecting, and all stirred up the aroma in my nostrils, the taste in my mouth and a glow I can still feel from nearly ten years ago."

Gregory handed her back the glass and sat on the arm of her chair. "You are a sensitive and warm woman, Sophie. Tell me about that memory," his voice softening almost to a whisper as he slipped his arm around her shoulders.

She tensed.

"Oh no, I couldn't, it's of no consequence to anyone but myself, anyway."

"I don't believe you," he persisted. "I do believe though, that you would feel a whole lot better if you shared some of those past moments."

She drew a quick breath.

His hand tilted her averted chin and she found herself drowning in the depth of his eyes. His thumb lightly sketched her trembling mouth and he considered her very closely in the half-light of the fire. She felt an ineffable warmth seeping through her as the wine took effect and she relaxed. His hand ruffled her hair. His touch was like a drug. Reluctantly she felt addicted, wanting more from him. She had a crazy desire to clutch him yet push him away from her, away from the danger zone. She closed her eyes, anticipating, as he leaned over her and gently lowered his mouth onto hers. It was a momentary kiss and she gave an involuntary moan as he moved his mouth across her cheek and she felt his warm breath, teasing her ear before he moved slowly to her mouth once more, only this time with a more pressing urgency as the throb of his lips caused her to groan with pleasure. He pulled way and quickly slipped off the arm of the chair. When he refilled his own glass, he eased himself into the chair opposite her.

"Now that you are more relaxed, what sensations did we conjure up with mulled wine?"

His voice was soft, cajoling. The wine warmed her and the gentleness of his touch had mesmerised her.

"Oxford," she replied, a dry feeling in her throat, as she tried to master control of herself again.

"You too?" his eyes held hers in a steady gaze.

"How do you mean, me too?"

"It's the traditional winter morning warmer in many colleges, my dear."

"Doesn't take much working out. You are very like your father."

"You knew him?"

"Professor Rayne was my pedagogue, mentor and guide for three years of my life," he raised his glass and an amused grin creased his face.

"You studied with him?" there was a catch in her voice as she smiled tremulously at him.

"A very clever historian, and a gentleman. Some of the best years of my life, and the most informative, were those days up at Christ Church …"

"I'm so happy you were able to know him." There was an immense pride in her voice. "Of course, as his daughter, I'm bound to say he was a very special person."

"You were close to him?"

"Very!" She felt the tears forming and turned to the fire.

"That explains so much, Sophie," his voice was barely audible.

For long moments, it seemed, she stared at the flickering flames. The crackling wood excited her and she watched the sparks.

"Robert and I used to imagine those sparks settling on the sooty back of the fire were armies, marching and obliterating each other as one fiery spark after another disappeared," she said distractedly.

"Robert?"

"My younger brother. He died in the accident with my father." She tried to sound matter-of-fact, but the dryness in her throat caused a tightness in her voice and she was afraid to look at him and show the tears welling up under her lids.

"I'm so truly sorry," he apologised. "I'd forgotten about your brother. Of course, your father kept his private life very private. To tell you the truth, I didn't even realise about your father's death. Not until I went to see your mother in Burnham Beeches. Well, that is, I knew of it, naturally, having read of it at the time, but one doesn't connect."

"Well, how did you know about the cottage?"

"A long story, and I'm not going to bore you with that one. However, I met your mother for the first time, I might add, although I had spoken to her on the telephone. I went to collect the keys and pay her for the cottage. Naturally, I saw the photo of your father on the wall in the lounge and the story fell into place. We talked for a long time then."

"When was that, Sophie asked, feeling an unjustified prickling irritation that he had been to see her mother and actually talked at length. She realised that her feelings were aroused by her own sense of guilt since she could not even remember when she had last given her mother enough of her own time and attention.

He did not reply.

"Did she mention me?" Sophie asked, a peculiar sense of resentment creeping over her.

"Briefly."

"What did she say? How was she?"

"She misses you," he replied tersely, rising to switch on the lights.

Sophie reddened with embarrassment and could find no words. She had neglected her mother badly and it rankled to have a stranger remind her of her failure to fulfil her filial duties.

Even at Christmas, they had only had a brief time together and that had been spent in the company of her aunt who was too possessive of her mother's company and had made Sophie feel like an outsider. Sophie reasoned that her work took her all over the country and it had been difficult to make time to be with her mother. There was no doubt Sophie had been selfish.

Gregory Markham must have been reading her thoughts.

"Don't worry about it, you can't be in two places at once. Besides, she has plenty to occupy herself just now." He sprawled in the chair opposite.

"What do you mean?"

He ignored her question, stretched himself and gave an exaggerated yawn. "How's about food, young lady? I've shown my talents, let's see what you can muster for a tired and hungry writer." He threw a couple of small logs onto the fire and settled back into the chair, lounging with his head tossed back, his dark eyes closed, suggesting he intended to doze while a meal was prepared.

Sophie disappeared into the kitchen and closed the door behind her. She felt more than slightly miffed at his attitude.

Since leaving Penzance he had made a calculated and successful attempt to discover her innermost feelings, scrutinise and assess her disposition. How easy and assailable she had proved to be, confiding in him in such a way. Now she regretted having revealed so much about herself and felt an angry swell rising in her against him. She knew she had only herself to blame. That was what made the situation worse. Her defence, her wall of privacy had been torn down, brick by brick, and now she was vulnerable. How foolish she had been to let him know anything at all about herself and the incident which had led her to the cottage.

Mechanically, trying to ride her own anger with herself, she began to prepare a meal, conscious of what she was doing, but churning her thoughts and actions over and over in her tired brain. The journey through the night, the friction of the day, the hassle with Lionel on the telephone, and then the warmth of the wine seeping through – it had diluted her defences and she had opened up to reveal too much of herself. Then, when she was at her most unguarded, Gregory had thrust in the knife wound of her relationship with her mother.

It was as if he had her at the point of a sabre and

she was without a weapon. At that moment, he had closed the contest and virtually despatched her into the kitchen.

Whether it was anger or frustration, she knew not, but the events of the last few days had brought her to tears and she let them have their rein. Silently, trickling down her cheeks as she stared out into the blackness, across the fields which sloped down towards the cliff tops.

It had a cathartic effect upon her and minutes later she was back to normal, putting the finishing touches to the meal. A hasty look in the kitchen mirror reassured her that her appearance gave nothing away, and she went back into the long room to lay the table.

She was aware that he was watching her every movement, although he said nothing, only moving to the table when she brought in the dishes of steaming spaghetti Bolognese. She was thankful she'd had the foresight to do some shopping in Penzance the first thing that morning before encountering Markham. For, despite what Willy Hoskins had told her about Mrs Tregarn bringing Markham's provisions to the cottage, there was certainly very little in the cupboards to have prepared a meal with anyway!

"Mm!" he sniffed approvingly, "I'm glad you added the garlic. I hoped you would, but of course I had no wish to come in and interfere in your culinary preparations."

She was thankful that he had not!

"First class, Sophie," he said, some time later, pushing his empty dish to one side and refilling both their empty glasses with the red wine he had brought to the table.

"I'm glad you approve," her voice was cool.

"So, you're talented beyond the realm of Research Assistant!" She suspected a sneer in his voice and rose to the occasion.

"Much valuable work is done by Research. Without it a lot of programmes would simply never get off the ground!"

"True," he agreed willingly. "What experience have you had?"

She reddened slightly, unsure if she should blow her own trumpet to such a degree, but at times he seemed to be patronising and she felt it might shake him to know she was no ordinary run of the mill researcher.

Whenever an interesting job had come up she had seized the opportunity thrust in her direction. In five years, she had worked in as many countries, gaining valuable experience and enjoying herself into the bargain. Last year, she had had an opportunity to return to Nigeria where, as a raw graduate of twenty-one, she had spent almost a year working with the Voluntary Service Overseas.

Her mother had been horrified that she was returning to 'that place'. "You'll be ill again," she had remonstrated, referring to the time when Sophie and five other VSO workers had been hurriedly flown back to an isolation unit with suspected Lassa Fever. They had been put in a plastic bubble in an isolation unit while tests were carried out.

Needless to say, it had all been a false alarm and because her time was nearly finished there anyway, they did not bother to fly her back. She was saddened that her time had ended so abruptly and regretted that she had been unable to return to make her proper farewells. She half suspected that, had she returned at that time, she would have stayed much longer and Fate would not have led her to reply to the advertisement for an 'enterprising, versatile, adaptable graduate, ready to travel at a moment's notice.' That had just been the start of a whole new life for Sophie.

She told Gregory Markham none of it. Let him think what he likes, she decided, and merely told him about the advertisement and how her life in TV had begun working for a few dreadful months on his low-key drama soap opera.

"You are scathing about my work," he sniffed.

She ignored his comment.

"I didn't let the grass grow under my feet – there wasn't much anyway, in 'High Rise'," she was delighted with her pun. "Then I worked as a Research Assistant and have encompassed programmes in comedy, education, drama, light entertainment, children's programmes, news, current affairs, documentaries and features. It's been a most rewarding five years."

"Hm," he acknowledged, nodding. "What do you know of Sheridan?"

"R B Sheridan?"

"The very same!"

"Not enough to write an essay." Her eyes met his.

"You won't need to – I've done all that part." He paused and his eyes narrowed, glinting with sharp interrogation. "Do you like him?"

"Is it important?" she asked stiffly.

"Up to a point, no, but … well, you may get more out of what I'm going to ask you to do if his work and life mean anything to you at all." There was a trace of impatience in his piercing eyes.

She looked towards the fire and swallowed noisily, perturbed by the intensity of his gaze and apprehensive over what he was about to ask her to do.

"Well?" he asked, a hint of irritation in his voice.

"From a historical point of view or literary?"

"Either."

"Well, from a literary standpoint I feel he burnt himself out without too much effort, although *School for Scandals* and *The Rivals* were not surpassed. That's my opinion, anyway. His treatment of Elizabeth Linley in the later years of their marriage would not have my recommendation, but from a historical point of view, I think he was an interesting and highly political character, despite the fact that he was misguided and unfulfilled." She turned to face him again and was taken aback to find him smiling and nodding with complete approbation.

"Well, so you *could* write an essay, and a damned good one too, Sophie!"

He leaned across the table and took her hand, gently playing with her fingers. He raised her hand and pressed his mouth to the softness of her palm. A sharp thrill ran through her. She slowly withdrew her hand.

He watched her closely, running his forefinger provocatively around the outline of his half-open mouth. There were glints of speculation in his eyes.

"Right now," he said huskily, "I'd like very much to make love to you."

Her mouth was dry and she felt an aching, tremulous sensation that was hard to ignore. Her pulse was racing and she was sure that the pounding in her chest must have been amplified ten times. The burning sensation at the back of her neck sent her giddy and lightheaded and seconds seemed like long minutes before he spoke again.

"However," he said, filling his glass with the last of the red wine, "I won't! There will be another occasion. Right now, I need to ask a favour of you."
Sophie could not reply. She felt a sense of relief as he moved towards the fire and sat back in the easy chair. At the same time, she was indignant at his attitude. "I won't, indeed, as if the choice was his!

"You've some holiday to take, right?" He looked deliberately at her.
She shrugged her shoulders. Lionel had, after all, advised her to take some leave.

"I won't beat about the bush, Sophie, how'd you feel about doing a spot of work for me for a while?"

"What sort of work?" She was intrigued.

"It would help us both out of a predicament."

"I'm not in one," she commented tersely.

"Oh, come on now, don't be difficult. You're at a loose end for two or three weeks – admit it."

"Not exactly, there are plenty of things I can do to occupy my time without you playing Employment Officer."

His voice was placatory. "I merely thought that, well, you've had an embarrassing and unpalatable experience. You may want to 'lie low' so to speak."
She stared at him.

"Look, I won't even be here, damn it! I shall be away. If you want to stay on here – it's your cottage, after all. You can type, can't you?"

"Of course I can!"

"That's where the Sheridan bit comes in." He

smiled, his eyes reluctant to leave, imploring her to show some interest and enthusiasm. "I normally never allow anyone to get near my work." There was a long pause. "I'd trust you," he offered magnanimously.

She was softened and swayed by his cajoling.

"So long as it's not your mawkish soap opera."

"I know better than to ask you to be involved in that. No! I've done a documentary – historical drama, really. It's quite finished, but requires a re-type for proof-reading purposes."

"What's stopping you from doing it yourself? If I hadn't arrived this morning, what would you have done anyway?" she asked perversely.

"Exactly! You've got me out of a huge predicament. Yesterday I had a letter from the publishers of something else that I'm working on – and that would undoubtedly interest you too – but that's another matter. At the same time, I've some final checking to do on some fine detail for the script of a film I've to have finished by next week. I need to get up to Plymouth."

"You need a secretary!" she responded dryly.

"I'll pay you," he proffered.

"Don't be so insulting!"

"I never meant to be – so you'll do it, then?"

"Well, I'll read it first and see – I don't want you pointing accusatory fingers afterwards."

"Right – I'll fetch it." He jumped from the chair and raced up the stairs two at a time, eager to fetch the manuscript before she changed her mind. By the time he returned, though, she had cleared away after dinner and even washed up. As he came down the stairs, she was sitting down with a coffee.

She said nothing as he thrust the manuscript into her hands.

"I'll see you later, then." He ignored the coffee, made no further comment and left the room, slamming the door behind him. She waited to hear the car start, but the crunch of his footsteps on the gravel began to fade. Clearly, wherever he was going was within walking distance.

It was nearly midnight when Sophie finished reading the manuscript. Markham had not returned, and assuming that he had a key with him, she went to bed. Considering the possibility that he might have gone to the Tin Mine Tavern to further lubricate himself, she took the precaution of locking her bedroom door.

It disturbed her that a man needed the stimulation of alcohol to produce such a masterpiece of drama like *Man of Vision*, the most absorbing drama she had read in a long time, revealing, amongst the sparkling wit and charm of an ebullient, optimistic nature, the character of a man who always seemed to be living 'on the fringe' of things. Richard Brinsley Sheridan was revealed as a man who turned the hardships of life into a joke.

Markham had written an extremely lengthy dramatization of Sheridan's life and clearly it was intended to be presented as thirteen scripts for television. Throughout the manuscript, he had indicated the ending for each episode and it would take her a considerable time to type out the work as a top copy for sending to his agent in London. But the work and the prospect of going through it excited her. She had sufficient vision and foreknowledge to anticipate the noises it would create in London. Period drama was much favoured and she mentally noted at least three directors who would be more than anxious to take on such a stimulating series. What Markham had revealed of Sheridan was the man with the quick brain which enabled him to tear out salient features of any problem and give the impression of knowing a subject in depth. This is the talent of the artist and indeed the playwright – to seize a quick impression of life, transfer it to stage or canvas and implant a fleeting feeling of the minds of others.

Markham had researched his character thoroughly and Sophie was left with a distinct admiration for Sheridan, despite the basic flaw in his character – a streak of vanity. After all, she reflected, a man is like a watch. All the pieces of the character are necessary to make the human being tick. And Sheridan was no exception with his easy sentimentality, suppressed tears, the horror of tragedy, the quick jibe and ready wit – each were part of the same man.

Her admiration for Gregory Markham too was increased, but she would not have been prepared to admit it to him.

## CHAPTER 4

The following morning Sophie agreed to do his work for him and suggested getting started on it right away.

"I think not – I've earned a day off," he said, a teasing gleam in his dark eyes as Sophie sat opposite him at breakfast. "I want you to join me," he added with a commanding tone.

Something in his voice made her stiffen against the suggestion.

"There's far too much typing here," she patted the manuscript lying on the chair beside her, "and considering I'm expected to do it on a clapped-out machine – it'll take simply ages!" she added ruefully.

"That typewriter has seen many good scripts and plenty more to come – I feel something familiar with that old machine every time I come back to it. It's like an old friend," he joked, knowing full well, but refusing to agree that it would take her half the time to reproduce his work on a more up-to-date electronic machine.

"I'll be lucky to have any fingertips left," she grinned.

"That's settled then," he started to move from the table. "We'll go in half an hour."

"Go where?" she demanded, "I've not agreed to

go anywhere."

He shrugged, his dark eyes resting on her, "I've agreed for you." His tone was emphatic.

"I'd like to make up my own mind, if you please," she protested, gathering the breakfast things together to occupy her mind and hands from the distraction of his penetrating gaze.

"Of course," he conceded, a note of cool mockery in his voice as he took the dishes from her and put them back on the table. In a quick second, he pulled her into his arms.

Her heart beat heavily in her ears as he pressed her into the hard length of his body. His lips brushed against her cheek as he murmured.

"This is not a seduction, Sophie, I merely want to spend the day with you – get to know you better. Do this little thing for me … please?" He turned her chin to look at her closely. There was something dark and disturbing in his eyes. Sophie felt she could drown in the suffocating sensuality of the man.

He released her as easily as he had taken her.

"Will you show me your favourite haunts?" he asked, "We only have today – come, it will be good for both of us, I promise," he coaxed.

Sophie found him irresistible but she knew she was standing at a door marked **Danger**. She was well aware she should not be entertaining thoughts of spending a day with a married man. But there was a feverish excitement racing through her and the magical intensity of anticipation as she chose to ignore the sign on the door.

The breathlessness of flirtation titillated sufficiently for her to avoid all caution signs. All sanity breathed cold air on her hot blood, but she allowed herself to be led by his perfectly disarming smile and winning words.

It was an agreeably warm day, for January, almost like Spring. A few ships were moving silently and imperceptibly across the bay, and far out on the horizon, Sophie had the faintest view of an ocean-going liner. The warm aroma from the bakery titillated her nostrils, cows were lowing in the meadow at the lower edge of the Carn and the children were arriving for another daily round at the tiny, grey stone school by the church.

"On such a day," Sophie admitted to Gregory, "I feel as if my place is *here*, for eternity."

As if the admission entitled him to intimacy, Gregory carefully took her arm and linked it through his possessively, drawing her close into him as they walked slowly along the lane that led down to the coast.

"And yet, there is a disturbing anonymity about it all," she continued easily. "Whatever happens, the cycle turns inevitably, just as it would, even if I were in London, Manchester, Oxford."

"Frightens you, does it?" he asked quietly, turning to look at her.

"Often. No-one would really be missed, would they? Oh, I know for a few days people's absence is noticed, but I mean long-term. Nothing or little would change." The prospect made her shudder and she gripped his arm involuntarily. Often, her thoughts, one moment so high, were suddenly in the next instant plummeted into the deepest despair at the enormity of the world and her tiny place in it.

"Paradoxical, isn't it? And do you realise why you have this ambivalence, Sophie?" Gregory asked, perfectly in tune with her mood and thoughts.

"I *thought* I did," she told him, baring confidences she had never revealed to anyone. "The joy and sheer ecstasy I feel at the one moment is just too much to be contained and … and well, there is never anyone with whom I can share it," she admitted.

"I know," he replied, "you feel you are in tune with the infinite and want to explode and proclaim it aloud."

"It seems an impossible task to compass the whole scene and retain it. It's a disappointment at my inability to preserve the moment, which evokes my despondency. I feel I want to encapsulate it forever – but it's impossible."

She stopped and looked out to sea.

"Beauty fades, don't you agree?"

"For a writer encapsulating with words, for the painter, the composer … well, you can, if you *feel* – you pass on the mood, the moment, the sensation and so on. That's what art is all about."

His arms went around her affectionately and they stayed that way for long moments cloaked in the euphoria that only two minds in harmony can feel, before Sophie broke away and, linking her arm in his quite unselfconsciously, she carried on walking along with him.

"Once, years ago, in Oxford," she admitted wistfully, "not long after … when my father and Robert were lost in the dinghy – I wrote it down then."

They walked along in silence for a while.

"Tell me," Gregory coaxed.

"Oh, it's nothing terribly clever, I'm afraid, but it was a feeling at the time – like you said – and I… I think I did get some kind of cathartic experience I suppose by trying to encapsulate my thoughts. It was a poem – I considered it so, anyway."

"Can you remember it?" he asked gently.

"Oh yes," she said wistfully, "it's always in my mind."

And she slowly began to reveal her poem to him.

*"Oh, we race through the days in our innocent ways*
*'cross grass moist with dew as we long for things new*
*And the trees seem to stare, all so leafless and bare*
*And they scorn as if to say*
*Who are you? Where are you going?*
*Don't you know you can't catch time?*
*And you will learn that you're ageing*
*With every minute that you climb*
*And each moment that you pass through*
*Has gone before it came*
*And the feelings that you had then*
*Will never be the same*
*For it's always then, it's never now*
*In the future we see when*
*We never touch it somehow"*

There was a long pause before he turned towards her.

"It's beautiful, Sophie – will you write it out for me when we get back to the cottage?"
She flushed awkwardly.

"It's not *that* clever!" she said embarrassed.

"I don't ask for *cleverness*, Sophie, but for sincerity and feeling. *You* should understand that." He kissed her lightly on the forehead. "Please do me a copy, won't you?"

"If you'd really like me to," she agreed, quite flattered.

"Now, where are you taking me? This is terrain you must know like the back of your hand."

"I do rather," she admitted, "so many, many holidays I've been here – I *feel* Cornish."

"I'd never been to this part of the country, Sophie, can you believe that?"

"Hush," she put a finger to his lips playfully, "don't let the pixies hear you!"

They were on the cliff top now and she pointed down to a small cove on the right.

"That's Boat Cove – my father had often taken the dinghy out from the Cove and the fishermen let him tie it up there, see, there's a tiny slipway. There's also a rather dilapidated hut too – as you can see – it's perched almost precariously on the cliff top I always expect to find it gone, blown away in the gales. Pushed up against the one side, there's one of those old-fashioned leather car bench seats – I've sat there for hours, reviving distant memories."

"Oh, Sophie," he said, tenderly, hugging her to him.

She experienced more warmth in those two words than she had felt in a long, long time.

As if from nowhere, though, on that lovely morning, a soft, seeping Cornish mist had started to hang over the sea threateningly.

"Unless the wind picks up," she told him, "that wretched mist can unfurl itself over the whole village in no time at all."

They had started to move back up the lane, for she wanted to take him past the disused mine and then back across the cliff top further round the coastal path to a place called Borlase Farm.

"Is that somebody's name?" he enquired keenly.

"No. Borlase literally means 'green summit', and Mr Trewellard, he's an ageless, gritty Cornishman who has farmed the cliff-top fields for fifty years or more, he maintained that he lived 'on top of the world'. It's aptly named though. I've often thought that in a high wind the outbuildings might be blown away out into the same Atlantic which whips and lashes against the cliffs in terrifying fury. Don't you think those icy green breakers look wicked, threatening to surge over the top of even a two-hundred-foot cliff top and take with them whatever lies in their path? And there it is," she pointed, "on the top, attempting to defy all, Borlase Farm, daring the relentless pounding of a merciless wind."

"Very descriptive!" he smiled.

Unfortunately, they never quite made it to the farm.

"Pity," she told him, he has delicious eggs – although how the hens survive the gales up here, heaven knows."

As she predicted, the mist, in its sudden vicious swirl, was coming all about them and they prudently decided to return to the cottage.

"An impregnable sanctuary," Sophie confessed.

"In more ways than one, I'm sure," he added, knowingly.

Despite Sophie's protestations Gregory determined on driving out for the rest of the day.

"I insist – besides, with this mist hanging about we'd be forced into each other's company right here in the cottage, and I'm afraid I couldn't be responsible for my actions!"

Sophie's reluctance evaporated. She had already

found herself enjoying his company too much. The merest touch from his hand excited her pulse rate too dramatically and the danger bells would ring on deafened ears.

The situation was altogether too easy to submit to the weakness of her own bodily needs.

She lay back in the comfort of his Rolls and idly asked where he intended driving, since he didn't know Cornwall.

"This one part, around Bodmin – I do know *that* area quite well, because ..." he stopped, obviously not intending to elaborate further.

As soon as they had left Penzance, the mists subsided and there was a watery sun trying to coax life on the cool day.

"I've got it in my mind to set a short historical drama down in this territory," Gregory told her as he accelerated up the A30.

"What kind of setting?"

"That's the trouble – something I'm not too familiar with I'm afraid – the sea – it would need a good researcher!" he added with a grin.

"Are you offering me a job?" she teased.

"No, seriously, it's part fact anyway – smuggling, and so on ..." he continued.

"But don't you think Daphne du Maurier and others have done it to death?" she interrupted.

"This is fact. One old smuggler, Wellard, his name, he was killed aboard his own cutter nearly two hundred years ago – a very undesirable lot!" he grinned quickly then turned his attention back to the road.

"I'd say you've spent too many nights in the Tin Mine Tavern in the village!" she chided humorously,

"I'll bet some of the old locals have tried to sell you a juicy tale – they all know who you are, you know," she added a laugh in her voice, "this place has its own bush telegraph – only down here they do it soundlessly, with gestures and nods!"

Suddenly he lapsed into an attempt at a Cornish dialect,

"All they little fishin' villages 'long the coast with tiny cottages an' fish cellars jumbled together – oh, yes, m'dear, they made excellent 'iding places for contraband. They stopped 'en, see. That would be 'bout in 1856 with the Coastguard Act they furriners passed up in London. The folks down 'ere took to bein' a bit more 'spectable, like. Still, there's a 'undred inlets round the coasts wi' names that remind folk of what used to go on. Places like Brandy Cove and Lucky 'ole. All the mystery's gone now and you don't 'ear the stealthy crunch of a boat beachin' at midnight, and murmuring voices. 'Tis a place for 'olidaymakers now, for picnics on the sand, an' children paddle in the pools an' explore the empty caves. Still, for those as was born 'ere, on misty winter evenin's, they might fancy they 'ear the phantom people in the coves, wi' their whisperin' shadows."

Sophie was enthralled.

"Not only write," she applauded, "you should play in it!" she added laughing.

"Perhaps you'll help me research it?" his question floated idly and she ignored it.

He took her to Jamaica Inn and they had a huge ploughman's lunch by a roaring log fire. In the afternoon they drove off into the strange, white world of the pyramids and pools that is the heart of the Cornish china clay industry.

For Sophie, the landscape had a strangely fantastic beauty all of its own. Spoil heaps of waste matter, shaped like pyramids, pointed towards a grey sky, great quarries formed around their bases and descended into immense pits filled with water, icy green like arctic pools in a frozen waste. There was a wild and magical grandeur like a lunar landscape. For centuries the Cornishmen had been wresting clay from this land, but there was nothing ugly about the old disused quarries and lakes. The land was not scarred and the white heaps stood like sentinels, as historic reminders to the countless generations who had, and would wrest a living from the granite.

They drove to Hensbarrow Downs, the highest point of this eerie lunar landscape and from there they could see the whole fantastic chain of white, conical monuments. Spreading to the west and then splaying out north and south, in seemingly indiscriminate heaps, looking rather like forbidding giant soldier-sentinels imperiously guarding the westerly tip of England against an invasion at the gateway to Cornwall.

But they *were* Cornwall, to Sophie, memorials, just as the remains of the old tin mines were reminders that the Cornishman, with daring and courage, despised an easy way of living.

The wind whipped around them, standing high on Hensbarrow Downs.

Sophie felt closer to Gregory Markham than she had ever been with any other man, apart from father. And that was a different kind of closeness, of course.

They turned to each other simultaneously and he brought his mouth down on hers, softly, pressuring slowly into a possessive force. His grip on her body was so firm and authoritative. When he took his mouth from hers, she said, "Gregory, I …"

"No, don't say anything, Sophie, not now," he urged, "I understand, believe me – I know … words are superfluous," he finished gently and then added, "there will be a time, I promise …" and he led her back to the warmth of the car.

For most of the journey back to the cottage they hardly spoke and just once he took her hand in his as he was driving and said, "Thank you for today, Sophie – you are like a breath of fresh air."

About eight o'clock that evening he left the cottage telling her not to wait up for him.

Sophie couldn't account for his mood change and was just thankful he would be leaving the next day. Today, she sighed, I have flirted dangerously with temptation – I must leave here as soon as I can.

## CHAPTER 5

Sometime during the early hours Markham must have returned, but he was quite obviously a man who required little sleep.

When Sophie awoke just after eight o'clock, she found that he had departed for Plymouth. His note on the dining table was polite, indicating his intention to be away for a few days and there was a hurried postscript, including a Surrey telephone number, 'PS. Any problems, contact Henry'.

She hoped that it would be unnecessary to introduce herself to Henry.

After a quick breakfast, she decided to set to work on the manuscript, carrying the old typewriter downstairs into the long room and putting it on the dining table. She had a particular aversion to sitting in Markham's improvised study, but she was even more exasperated to find that he had not left her sufficient paper to type the manuscript. To complete the work she would need at least two more reams of paper. She would have to take it into town to produce a photocopy.

It frustrated Sophie when minor disruptions occurred to upset her plan of things, and it was with an ill will that she drove to the stationers in Penzance. There was no telephone at the cottage – it had been agreed that the last vestige of privacy should remain, and the village 'phone was out of action, so whilst in Penzance she took the opportunity of calling her mother. But there was no reply. She let the number ring out for some minutes and then had the operator check the number. Strange for her mother not to be at the bungalow. It irritated her when things did not just fall into place at the time she wanted and she set off back to the cottage.

Just out of Penzance she turned off right up Mount Misery taking the St. Just Road. Halfway up the hill, something prompted her to pull into the side of the road and stop the car. She drew her thick jacket around her and got out to take a look at the magnificent view of the tiny fortress island off Marazion, which had dominated Mount's Bay. This view of St. Michael's Mount never failed to excite Sophie and cause her to wonder why Mount Misery, with such a splendid aspect, had been so named.

For a moment, she was oblivious to the harsh wind that curled around her collar as she was transported back to a warm, Spring afternoon, years previously, when her father had taken them all on a trip, the first of many, across from the mainland, in his dinghy. They had climbed the rocky path, where flowers seemed to grow in profusion everywhere. Masses of hydrangea and flowering fuchsia had succeeded the ranks of rhododendrons and the more fragile flowers of early spring. Her father's voice purred in her receptive ears,

"And we came to the isle of Flowers, their breath met us out on the seas,

For the Spring and middle Summer sat each on the lap of the breeze."

For her, like so many others, no doubt, St. Michael's Mount was one of the most romantic sights in England, and not just Tennyson's imagined isle.

They had returned many times, she and her father alone, to sate themselves in the atmosphere. Benedictine monks, feudal barons and rebellious earls had looked across to the mainland a thousand times before her. Traditions of the Mount reached to the dark mists of time when Phoenicians had sailed to barter their fine cloth for Cornish tin. The Mount was a place where for centuries a population of a thousand people, fishermen and traders had survived through all the storm and stress which had assailed the Mount through most of its years. It had been the stronghold of fighting men and warrior priests, and with her father she had heard the tramp of armed feet on the stones and walls echo with the clash of steel.

Those were the magic days when her father had stirred up a deep and abiding interest in the past within her. It had led along many paths since and little had she realised that indirectly it would bring her back down to Cornwall on this cold, January morning.

She sighed for all that *had* been and a lump came to her throat as she thought again of her father, and all that *might* have been.

When the smashed dinghy had finally been washed ashore, some years later, with her mother she had been called to identify the remains in Penzance. The bodies had never been found, but the poignancy of her mother's words echoed, "Now he'll never write his books." It had been a foolish and empty statement at the time, but on many occasions in the last years, Sophie had no doubt just what a goal he had set himself. After the accident, they had moved from the house just outside Oxford to a small bungalow at Burnham Beeches, so that her mother could be nearer to her own sister. While they were packing, Sophie came upon reams of notes, meticulously written in exercise books, each carefully annotated, dated and with various references and sources for further notes. There were thirty of them!

"I don't want to throw them away," her mother had sentimentally remarked, "who knows, one day you might pick up where your father left off."

It had been too soon, then, and she was too close to her father to so much as look at his handwriting without shedding tears. Besides, she had another two years to do at University. She was glad, at least, that her father had seen her achieve her place at Oxford. He had been more than partly responsible, of course, tutoring her at every opportunity, stimulating her interest in academic study, advising her on the best books to read, improving her mind and developing her questioning nature.

They had spent hours together in Blackwells in Oxford – "the best bookshop in the world," he had said, and she believed him, for he always talked with such authority and experience. As a member of the University himself he had been anxious to encourage her to attempt for entry. She had never even considered herself clever enough to succeed, but her father was convinced she was capable and that became enough for her.

She had always been closer to her father than her mother, although the death of her father had meant that Sophie had drawn nearer to her mother. She had not wanted to move out of Oxford, especially as it meant she would have to live in College all term, but she knew just how deeply her mother was affected by the sight and sound of everything in Oxford. The loss of her husband was grief enough to bear, but losing Robert had doubled the pain. If only he had not gone with his father that morning she would at least have some masculine reminder to grow into manhood. Robert had been very precious to all of them. A small, stocky boy of fourteen, he was a perfect replica of his father, right down to his gold-rimmed spectacles and his gentle, caring nature. He did not have his father's love of history, however, and this was probably why Sophie had taken such a special place in her father's heart.

As she got back into the car she reflected that Robert would probably just have finished University, if he had lived. What a waste!

By lunchtime she was back at the cottage and very busy at the typewriter. All her frustrations and exasperations with Markham were dissipated as she was able to experience the joy of his writing once again. She became totally absorbed in his manuscript. She had a great respect for the clarity of his text, and although she was no authority on drama scripts, she had plenty of experience in research to convince her of the subtlety of his style and the structuring of his work.

For Sophie, the first part of the script she typed had more than particular historical significance, for it revealed that Sheridan and his new wife, Elizabeth Linley, honeymooned at East Burnham, close to her own home at Burnham Beeches, and in fact lived there for a year. Despite the twentieth century encroachment, the beech and oak woods, interspersed with narrow twisting lanes, were very much the same as in the eighteenth century, and although the name of the cottage they had lived in had disappeared, she was not unfamiliar with Pumpkin Hill and East Burnham Well!

Sophie was beginning to feel very tired. She scarcely stopped working in the eight hours, and then only to take a light snack. Markham's typing was not difficult, but continually throughout the manuscript he had made extensive alterations in the most appalling handwriting which at times she had found almost impossible to decipher. It had taken her much longer, therefore, to produce the first two episodes into top copy. She put another log on the fire, made herself a mug of coffee and curled in the capacious armchair by the fire.

This was not how she had planned to spend her time away from the world of television, but it had certainly taken the sting out of the circumstances which had caused her hasty departure from Manchester. She had been more disappointed to find her mother not at home when she had telephoned earlier. Somehow it seemed necessary to verify that Markham *had* rented the cottage – it would have been more positive proof than pinching herself as reassurance that this whole farcical situation was really taking place. However, it would enable her to take stock of things – something she rarely had time to do during the normal course of events.

One of the main elements about her job which had so much appeal was the quickness with which the situation could change and boredom never had a chance to set in. There was a consistent variety of work, particularly when she had worked on a magazine programme. In one week, she had been involved in an item on Einstein, Greenpeace and their intervention at a whaling campaign, an investigation into witchcraft, and a look at the crazy cult of 'bottle digging' on Victorian salvage sites. She had met many different people and travelled to places which she would probably never have visited if she had not responded, all those years ago, to an advertisement which had certainly lived up to its expectations!

The doorbell rang just as Sophie was preparing a lunch-time snack on the Friday.

Willie Hoskins handed her a telegram.

"Shouldn't rightly be 'andin' it to you – seein' as 'ow it's not addressed to you, but I reckon it'll be alright."

Twenty minutes later she was still debating whether or not to open Markham's telegram. She had only met the man a few days previously, prepared him food, slept under the same roof, spent a whole day jaunting around Cornwall with him, agreed to type his manuscript – opening the telegram seemed a minor offence in comparison to everything else!

*ARRIVING PENZANCE FRIDAY PM*
*PLEASE MEET TRAIN URGENT*
*PENELOPE*

Sophie was not a person inclined to panic, but on this occasion it would be wrong to assume that a measure of agitation had not come over her. Too late to stop the woman from arriving – she would have boarded the train in London, judging by the address indicated on the telegram.

Henry!

She found Gregory Markham's note from under

the pile of paper on the table and looked closely at the telephone number where she could locate the Miracle man, Henry. She doubted he would be able to do very much, considering he was based in Surrey, Markham had gone to Plymouth and Mrs Markham would be arriving in Penzance in a couple of hours! It was worth a try!

She left everything just as it was, grabbed her coat and car and keys and sped off to Penzance.

There was no reply from Henry's number.

It had started to drizzle, she had had no lunch, the train was due in at three o'clock and the Buffet Bar on the station was closed. She left the car and walked along the harbour to the Bus Station Café.

With a cheese sandwich and a rather murky looking cup of tea, she sat down to wait for the inevitable embarrassment which would ensue from the arrival of the London train. *That* part of the dilemma had only really hit her when she found Henry not at home. Her confidence had raced away like a spring flood.

"Any problems, contact Henry." That had looked most reassuring scrawled on Markham's note. Who was he, anyway? She immediately thought of a bloodhound and Clement Freud, the politician who had frequently propounded the merits of a certain brand of dog food. A momentary vision of a rotund, balding man with a disappearing chin and large, fat, sweaty hands sprang to mind.

How cruel! The imagination can run riot, she reflected. Henry was probably a twenty-five-year-old whizz kid accountant who kept all Markham's finances in check. She smiled at her pun. Beyond this musing, it dawned on her that she was, herself, in rather an invidious position.

Penelope, intent upon a quiet and private, but urgent, weekend would arrive to find him absent, having left an unknown and unattached female ensconced in his rented West Country retreat. If any situation could be misconstrued, then this was it. To attempt to explain away the peculiar set of circumstances which had led to Sophie's presence at Penzance station was even more reminiscent of a scene from one of Sheridan's comedies!

Sophie could only laugh at the state of affairs because it was so unreal. But she *did* have pangs of guilt for the cosy day she'd spent with Gregory on the drive to Bodmin. The average, normal, level-headed female does not walk out on her job, drive six hours through a winter night to a lonely cottage at the far-westerly tip of Cornwall, only to find it inhabited by an erudite playwright who just happens to be in need of a typist on that cold, January afternoon.

It would be unlikely then that the same healthy, respectable female would accept the offer of a stranger's hospitality, sleep under the same roof, cook his meals and then calmly meet his wife a few days later, and expect the wife to take the situation well within her stride.

Sophie assumed 'Penelope' was 'the wife' and doubted whether Mrs Markham would appreciate the legitimacy of the situation and as the train pulled into the station, she visualised the headlines branding her as the dissolute and libertine mistress of Gregory Markham, detected in a Cornish love-nest by his guileless and trusting wife!

It was a situation which hardly augured well for a satisfactory evening, but Sophie had little choice in suggesting that Mrs Markham stay at the cottage.

All the explanations were over and Sophie was quite aware that Mrs Markham, as she had imagined, had found them less than credible and placed her own interpretation on the events which had been related to her. She did not disclose her feelings verbally, but it was apparent from the ungracious manner and the facile smile that she was more than a little disconcerted and making every possible attempt to disguise her displeasure.

Mrs Markham had been silent on the drive from Penzance and Sophie, to be fair, tried to place herself in the unfortunate woman's position. On the face of it, it did seem an implausible story. To think that she, whose mother owned the cottage, was unaware that her mother could have rented it out, and arrived quite out of the blue on a cold winter's day, having never met Gregory Markham, stayed on and became his temporary typist. Yes, Sophie reflected, the poor woman must be fuming inside, desperately trying to appear unruffled and polite.

"Whatever possessed Greg to hide away in this place, I can scarcely imagine," Mrs Markham grimaced as Sophie pulled up in front of the cottage. "'Chy-an-Weal', funny name for a place – does it have any particular significance?"

"It means 'the house on the mine'," Sophie replied coolly, quite affronted. "But you'll be quite safe," she reassured her sarcastically, observing the look of absolute horror on Mrs Markham's face, "the cottage had stood for two hundred years and the mine is a thousand feet or more below the surface. There are miles of labyrinthine tunnels below this part of the Cornish coastline."

"What sort of mines?"

"Why, tin, of course," Sophie retorted shortly, getting out of the car.

The woman irritated her. It was natural for Sophie to defend the family cottage from those who make disparaging remarks, but her irritation went deeper. She felt she had put herself out for the woman, and because she had, in her own eyes, done nothing wrong, apart perhaps from imprudently arriving without first checking with her mother, it caused her to resent the insinuation of the woman's silence.

Even the day out with Gregory had been quite without any 'naughty' event. You can't charge someone for having licentious thoughts, she reflected, remembering how receptive her mind had been to certain statements and suggestions made by Gregory Markham! Sophie could, and perhaps should, have elaborated for Mrs Markham, but when she had mentioned telephoning Henry, there had been a snort of derision in the woman's response to Sophie's well-meaning endeavours.

There was no suggestion as to how long Mrs Markham had come for, and indeed why she had come, although Sophie accepted that it was absolutely none of her business. She was grateful for one thing at least. Mrs Markham was as taciturn as her husband was garrulous. Whether this was her normal manner or a result of the improbable and unpalatable circumstances in which she found herself, was debatable, but it enabled Sophie to continue uninterrupted with the typing of the Sheridan manuscript. It was also one palpable proof that at least *some* of her explanations to Mrs Markham had been correct. However, while she was typing, she heard Mrs Markham verifying the rest of the story as far as possible as she creaked across the floorboards above and surreptitiously tried all the doors, obviously looking in the remaining bedrooms for confirmation of some kind. Sophie could hardly object. Gregory Markham had, after all, paid the rent and his wife had every right to inspect the property.

When they had arrived at the cottage, Sophie had offered to prepare food, but Mrs Markham had declined, saying she had eaten on the train from London and asked only to be shown "somewhere where I might lay my weary head."

"Your husband uses this room to sleep in," Sophie had said indifferently, and left Mrs Markham to minister to her own needs. She had also shown her the bathroom, which of course was on the ground floor.

Penelope Markham was considerably older than in the photograph which Sophie had seen in Gregory's 'study', although she was cleverly made up to assume the subtle disguise of a woman in her late twenties. The style and cut of her clothes divulged much of her expensive taste in dress and she manifested an air of affluent superiority. She had accepted all the explanations with the quiet calm of one who believes that silence is the best answer to the fool.

Although Sophie didn't like the woman's supercilious nature, she admired the cool dignity in not asking probing questions like a haranguing fishwife. She had met plenty of people like Mrs Markham throughout her working life, and had come to the conclusion that such people are either extremely well-bred or first-class thespians.

She was not an unattractive woman and had obviously made considerable effort to retain her youthful figure, despite the ravages of motherhood and playing wife to someone as histrionic and saturnine as Gregory Markham appeared to be.

Her rather too-thin mouth had been cleverly made up to give the appearance of a more sensuous outline and Sophie, who preferred to look people straight in the eye when talking to them, found her cold and expressionless. There was a distant emptiness which belied the artificial sensuality of the mouth and when Sophie spoke to her, she had averted her eyes and merely nodded a response to Sophie's suggestion that Henry might have some knowledge about her husband's movements and his likely return to the cottage.

It was almost a snort of disapproval which Sophie found quite out of character. With an air of weary detachment, she had carried her overnight bag upstairs as if this whole tasteless situation was quite beneath her. In a way, Sophie was relieved with the outcome of the meeting, for she had been more than apprehensive, under the circumstances, with visions of an outraged wife and the possibility of indecorous wrangling on the latter's part, filled with unjustified and libellous accusations.

If that *had* happened, Sophie would simply have packed her suitcase and driven off from the cottage. She deplored argument and hassle and had a strong abhorrence of discord in any form. Now she would be able to set to and finish the manuscript as she had promised, but if there *were* to be any trouble with Mrs Markham, she would take the whole thing and complete the job in London and then send it on to Gregory Markham. The latter seemed such a good idea, she couldn't think why she had not considered it before.

It was nearly midnight when she finished typing and went up to bed. Her guest had not reappeared in all that time and she had felt indisposed towards calling her since it would have delayed her work. Besides, she reasoned, the woman had a tongue in her head, and was quite capable of looking after herself.

The typing had been effortless because she found the content so absorbing, and although Sophie would not have admitted it to the author, she *did* feel honoured to have had this preview of a remarkable piece of work. It must have taken him months, apart from all the research. Little wonder that he had buried himself away from his wife and family. S

he was curious to know what had brought his wife hurrying to the cottage and even more so because it was obvious that she was not informed of all her husband's whereabouts and movements, otherwise she would not have made the abortive visit. Markham had intimated he would be away for a few days, and in a writer's terms that could mean at least a week! The prospect of entertaining his wife for that length of time palled.

It was important to have contingency arrangements, should Mrs Markham indicate her intention to stay at the cottage. The manuscript could quite easily be finished by the Saturday evening if Sophie was uninterrupted. She had already completed nine of the episodes which had taken Richard Sheridan into a lively and interesting political life in the House of Commons and as a member of the

Cabinet. Markham had adroitly revealed the character of Sheridan as a man who was only himself when he was *not* himself, a man with that strange, amorphous quality required by an actor – the ability to take on the protective colouring of a different character. Significantly, he had not failed to include Sheridan's improprieties, indicating there was no doubt he was unfaithful to Elizabeth, but in an age when male infidelity was regarded as a peccadillo, and part of a man's life beyond the home, this was not perhaps the worst damage which Richard Sheridan was doing to his chances in life. It was at that point in the work that Sophie had stopped.

Apart from the fact she had completed episode nine, it had reminded her of the very reason why she was sitting at midnight in a Cornish cottage typing the manuscript of a man who appeared to have a very peculiar relationship with his wife. None of my business, she reasoned, turning off all the lights, but it sickened and disgusted to her to think that men always seem to get away with the double standard. It determined her to finish the typing on the following day and leave for London, come what may.

The light was on in Mrs Markham's room and Sophie was tempted to knock and ask if she required anything, but her better judgement prevailed and ignoring the light, she settled herself in her own room and was soon asleep.

"I wonder if I might prevail upon you to take me into Penzance, Miss Rayne?" came the cool request as Sophie appeared at the top of the spiral stairway.

It was before eight and Sophie, in dressing gown and slippers, was somewhat disconcerted as she sleepily emerged to make herself an early cup of coffee preparatory to breakfast.

"What, now?" there was a hint of aggression in Sophie's voice.

"Preferably in time to catch the London train," came the acid retort.

"But you've …"

"Would you be good enough, young lady, not to try and interpret my actions, as I am sure I am not in any way answerable to *you*. I have the ability to appraise a situation very quickly and my decision to return to London as soon as possible can be effected the more readily if you are in a position to drive me to Penzance."

It was on the tip of Sophie's tongue to mention the name of the local taxi driver but she restrained herself. The distant, cold, supercilious tone incensed Sophie, who was still at the top of the stairs and so taken aback that she was quite unable to deal with such hostility and promptly turned back into her bedroom. It was one thing to have a contingency plan, but this form of attack had completely caught her off her guard. She had not for one moment imagined that Mrs Markham would want to depart with such alacrity. Just how long she had been sitting in the chair waiting for Sophie was impossible to gauge.

Sophie admitted defeat. The most satisfactory solution was to take the wretched woman to her train and the sooner the act was accomplished, then the sooner she could get on with her work. Nothing would be achieved by attempting to reason with Mrs Markham and she was convinced that as soon as the woman was out of sight she would be out of mind. She had long ago developed the art of shutting out all around her and concentrating on her own thoughts or work.

Five minutes later, fully dressed, Sophie came down the stairs, collected her coat and car keys and went out to start up the car. Mrs Markham made no attempt at a conversation all the way into the station and Sophie had already mentally blocked the woman from her thoughts, so even if she had spoken to her, it was unlikely that she would have responded. She pulled up sharply in front of the station drive.

Without a word on either side, Mrs Markham slammed the car door and Sophie drove back to the cottage.

By the time she was eating her breakfast and warmed herself with coffee, the woman was far from her thoughts, although it had crossed her mind that a train from London would not depart until well after lunch and Mrs Markham would have a long, cold, disagreeable wait in the draughty waiting rooms.

In her haste to leave Mrs Markham and get back to the cottage, she had neglected to telephone Henry. A bit late for that now, she reflected, popping more buttered toast into her mouth.

At some time during the morning Willy Hoskins arrived with a letter from Gregory Markham. One sheet of notepaper with the minimum amount of information.

"Sophie – it is necessary for me to go direct up to London. I will return by mid-week. I am in your debt! Gregory."

There was no date, simply a Plymouth postmark, first class, dated Friday. Perhaps Mrs Markham was psychic!

Sophie had no intention of waiting for his return. Although she was someone who revelled in excitement and change, she still preferred things to be fairly straightforward, and the type of situation she was in could hardly be described as that. It was important to have prescribed parameters in which to work – and play, for that matter!

She felt she had spent too much valuable time pondering the peculiar proclivities of the Markhams.

By Monday morning, having taken a slightly more leisurely approach to the work, knowing that Markham's return was not so imminent, she completed the typing of the manuscript.

Sophie felt that she owed Gregory Markham nothing.

Leaving a short note and the completed manuscript behind her in the cottage, she drove back to London and the privacy of her own flat.

# CHAPTER 6

Amongst all the post which had accumulated at the flat over the last weeks was a card from her mother informing her that she was taking a 'short winter break' with a 'friend'. No wonder Sophie hadn't been able to contact her mother on the 'phone. Turning the card over, imagining her mother to be at some tried and trusted boarding house in Torquay, she was flabbergasted to find an exotic view of Sunset Club, Senegambia. She didn't believe it! It was some sort of joke!

Her mother, who was a shy, retiring, almost reclusive type of person during the last few years, had apparently taken a winter holiday in West Africa with a 'friend'. The fact that her mother had put the word in inverted commas gave rise to all manner of possibilities in Sophie's mind. As far as she knew, her mother had scarcely any friends that she would be likely to spend a holiday with. Her immediate reaction was to ring her aunt and find out more, but she recollected the latter's hostile attitude to her at Christmas and sensed that a 'phone call would only give her aunt cause to gloat. That was assuming that her aunt knew anything about it, of course.

Sophie's only real knowledge of Gambia was the Abuko Nature Reserve. Years ago, when she had been on the VSO, she had met Duncan Armstrong, then recently qualified as a veterinary surgeon, and during their stay in Nigeria he had told her of Abuko. It had a reputation as being one of the finest reserves in West Africa, spread over hundreds of acres of tropical forest and savannah, with exotic Bamboo Pool, where crocodiles abound. The whole area was filled with snakes, antelope, monkeys and many species of birds. She had intended to fly back to the UK with Duncan via Gambia, but of course their untimely departure from Nigeria with Lassa fever had thrown their plans to the wind.

And now, her mother, who had once thrown her hands up in horror when Sophie had told her she would be returning to Nigeria with a TV film unit, and who up to now had never left England, was soaking up the tropical splendour.

In one of the side streets off Shaftesbury Avenue, Sophie eased her way amongst the theatre crowds to a tiny restaurant that held the promise of good food and a quiet dinner.

Sophie, who prided herself on coping with life's dilemmas, and always so perfectly at ease in her own company, had felt desperately lonely and thrown off-balance. She had intended to spend some time with her mother, perhaps go away for a few days, but she suddenly felt on the fringe of her mother's life, as if she had been excluded from something vital.

She had no right to expect anything from her mother in that respect and since her own way of life had continued with barely a consideration for her mother, then there was even more reason. Gregory Markham had been rather pointed about it and had caused her to have serious feelings of guilt. Sitting alone in her flat that evening she had realised that, apart from her job, there was very little in her life these days. Her social life was practically non-existent, partly through lack of time and because she was ever unwilling to share herself too readily. She had very few friends on whom she could call at a moment's notice and fill an odd hour. Because of the fact that she had scarcely been at the flat for weeks, working in Manchester and only popping home some of the weekends, there was nothing too interesting in the food line in the kitchen cupboards, and she had decided to take herself into town and indulge in a meal.

"Most people go out to dinner with a partner," a broad, but soft Scots accent broke in on her thoughts as she began her sweet of pineapple cheesecake.

"Duncan Armstrong!" she squealed with delight, jumping up and sending the cutlery flying across the table. "Oh, Duncan, how lovely to see you. I thought you were in Argyllshire? You were marrying Vanessa. How is everything? What are you doing here?!" She scarcely stopped for breath.

He hugged her with a warmth and vigour that quelled all her previous despondency.

"One question at a time. Oh, yes, you're about the same, Sophie, no time for breath! Och, lass, can I join you?"

During the next hour, Sophie let Duncan explain about his marriage with Vanessa being over, not least of the reasons being because he had turned vegetarian and her wealthy father had established a deer farm and expected his son-in-law to run it! There had been minor infidelities on both sides, too, but they had both agreed that the marriage was over.

"And the divorce?" she queries.

"That's another thing, that's got me damned mad!" he said evasively, filling their wine glasses. "She even settled a considerable sum of 'Daddy's' money on me," he added scathingly. "I'm expected to disappear now – she's to come out of all this like sugar icing. I'll be a few thousand better off, though. They've so much money, it's nothing short of obscene."

"Duncan, I'm so very sorry. But what are you going to do now?"

"I'm about to leave for Kenya. I've landed myself a very plum job – it's not that well-paid, but the quality of the job is right for me – I'm going to be assigned to a Safari Park. At least they don't breed to kill!" he added ruefully.

It seemed a perfectly natural suggestion for Sophie to offer the spare room at the flat to Duncan. Temporarily ensconced in a hotel while waiting to fly out to Kenya, he jumped at the opportunity, and the following morning appeared, bag and baggage, at her flat as arranged.

Since she was on 'leave of absence', they had plenty of time at their disposal and for the next week or so enjoyed each other's company in an almost dissolute fashion. Duncan was quite happy to 'blue' some of Vanessa's money and they ate out each evening after a long day of sight-seeing, reckless shopping sprees for things he might need in Africa and endless meanderings around the city.

For Sophie, it was a time to repair herself emotionally and gain her self-confidence – a time to trust the opposite sex. With Duncan, it was possible to feel like a woman cossetted without being courted.

He conducted himself always as a master of propriety and courtesy.

One evening, nearly two weeks later, dining at Chez Solange in Cranbourne Street, she toasted his imminent departure with tears of regret in her eyes.

"Och, Sophie, I wouldn' ha' traded these past days for anything. I only have the one regret ..." his voice trailed off sadly, and he willed her to turn her eyes towards him in the silence of seemingly long moments which followed. "I'd like to take you with me."

He swallowed noisily and she was only too aware of the emotion which Duncan was suppressing.
She reached slowly for his hand and smiled wanly as she twined her fingers in his.

"You know, Sophie, I've had to contain a lifetime of wanting with you this last couple of weeks. I can tell you now because ..."

"Please, don't," she begged, quietly in the crowded restaurant.

"No, I must say what I feel," he pressed. "You're a fine woman, Sophie. I've always respected you – that's ma damned trouble!" he laughed awkwardly. "Ma God, the man who gets you is to be envied. Don't think badly of me – I had to tell you. I'm crazy for you. Perhaps it's as well I'm going away – unless you'd come?" he pleaded.

"Duncan, I ..." Sophie attempted, but a lump came to her throat and she looked way. Long moments passed and he refilled her champagne glass, before she was able to continue. "Write to me – thrown together like we have been again, I'm sure of many things, but ..." she faltered to a stop, reddening as her heart quickened insensibly. Gregory and Mrs

Markham had walked into the restaurant.

It was immediately obvious that Markham had seen her and although the waiter attempted to direct them to an apparently reserved table, he made straight for Sophie and Duncan, steering his wife unerringly through the narrow passages between the tables without taking his gaze from Sophie.

There was no avoiding the confrontation and Sophie, embarrassed and uneasy throughout, was relieved to find Mrs Markham's hitherto icy attitude considerably warmer. Perhaps she felt less threatened seeing Sophie with Duncan. Whatever the reason, it was clear that Mrs Markham's hostility toward her had abated and when Gregory suggested that he and his wife join them, Duncan, in true, warm, Scottish spirit, was only too pleased to welcome Sophie's acquaintances with a readiness which she felt sure he would have reserved had he known her true feelings towards Gregory Markham!

She had had plenty of opportunity on the long drive from Cornwall to London to reassess her situation. She knew why she had left the cottage in a hurry. In a few short days with Gregory, and, indeed, in the few short days without him, through his ebullience and quick temper, his gentleness and remonstrances, through his presence and lack of it, and finally through his sensitivity as a writer, she knew she wanted him and she would have no control over herself to resist him. He left an aura of his presence, despite her attempts to avoid its overpowering influence. His wife's appearance at the cottage had been a timely life-saver to her.

Adultery and affairs disgusted her sense of righteousness. But even the strongest of characters finds the chemistry of feeling between two people so overpowering that, at the moment of transgression, morals cease to exist. Though emotionally bright, she was emotionally naïve and the intensity of feeling was powerful and hard to control. Sophie had been thankful for breathing space in those moments with Gregory Markham.

For once in her short life, she had met an intellectual equal who had excited her, stimulated her and whom she craved physically. In the cold moments of awareness, the fact that he was another woman's husband offended her sense of decency. She was ashamed of her licentious thoughts.

All those miles, driving alone, remembering the terse note she had left him back at the cottage, she had tried to win the argument with herself over the moral precepts which had been so much a part of her upbringing. Her father, her dear father ... she would never have been able to face him. He had been such an upright man. His code of conduct for life, in all things, had been irreproachable.

She could not fail to be touched by the irony too! The man she had fallen for had held her father in such high regard in his own student days.

"I leave as I entered – suddenly! Good luck with 'A Man of Vision' and thank you for letting me have a preview."

How she regretted now the empty, tasteless note she had left for him.

But tonight, Gregory was a different man, another character from the one she had known in Cornwall. There was almost an obsequious strain to him. He agreed with everything they said, smiled freely, was disarmingly polite and friendly without a trace of the sudden moments of emotion she had encountered at the cottage. Throughout the meal they shared, she felt his eyes scarcely left her. He was careless to a point of disinterest with his wife, who appeared not to notice his attitude or was accustomed to his behaviour.

He even agreed with Duncan on certain issues, which surprised her, for as the evening wore on and Markham drank more wine with his dinner than the others, he began to carry the look of a predator. So little was said of the Cornish adventure and although Duncan knew that Sophie had spent some days with Markham at the cottage, he had little suspicion of her true feelings.

Nothing was said of Mrs Markham's peremptory visit, either, and Sophie began to wonder if the whole adventure had been a tasteless dream.

Before they parted, Gregory hinted at the already raging approval of 'Man of Vision'. She was delighted for him and as they shook hands on parting, a strange ineffable warmth invaded her body.

Dryly in desperation she attempted a genuine congratulatory comment and in an unseen moment he pressed his forefinger to her lips in a significant gesture. As they all parted he made a laudable speech of friendship, his eyes reluctant to leave her, and Sophie wondered how much the others had been aware of Gregory's attention towards her.

# CHAPTER 7

As her eyes slowly began to open, Sophie struggled to focus on the unfamiliar surroundings of the hospital room. A strange voice murmured urgently and she heard footsteps. A door closed and seconds later, re-opened and she became conscious of a short, spectacled man in a white coat, moving, almost gliding towards her. She felt she must be coming round from an anaesthetic and attempted to raise her head, finding it impossible, as if her body was strapped down to the bed. There was a tight, dry soreness in her throat and a pounding sensation in her head.

The room seemed too bright. It was easier to close the eyes and sink back into the mindless, timeless, effortless state of sleep. But there were people all around her bed now, sounds of activity, voices urging her to life and resentfully, she struggled to waken only to have a torch shone in her half-open eyes.

She felt as if she was being winched up, and looking down towards her feet saw the bottom half of her body being lowered whilst the rest of her was brought up into a sitting position.

Both her legs were encased in plaster and dangling forlornly in a complicated structure of slings and pulleys at the end of the bed. Even her neck was trapped in a rigid plastic collar which seemed to flow down her left arm, which was also encased.

"The Sergeant would like to ask you a few questions, Miss Rayne. Do you feel up to it just yet?" She blinked hopelessly.

"I'm afraid he'll have to wait a little longer, nurse," the same voice turned to the blue-coated woman at his side. "Show her young man in, will you, that might help her round more quickly."

"Water, please … can I have some water?" Sophie begged, the soreness of her throat becoming quite unbearable. She tried to lift herself but it was impossible. Without a word the doctor placed a small beaker to her lips and allowed her only a few drops.

"Mustn't let you be sick, now, Miss Rayne," he commented.

"What's happened to me?" her voice rasped.

"Nothing that we can't put right, Miss Rayne," the doctor avoided looking at her. "Ah, now here's your young man, that'll go a long way to mending you, I'm sure," he turned on his heel and left the room.

"Och, Sophie, ma wee precious, how are you feeling?" My God, I can hardly see you in all the trappings," he attempted a laugh.
Partly through fear and partly through self-pity, she began to cry. Both her arms were trapped in plaster and slings and she felt totally defenceless.

Duncan let her cry. He wanted desperately to hold her to him and ease her distress but she was untouchable in her discomfort at that moment.

"Duncan, oh Duncan, what happened to me?" she sobbed.

He leaned over the bed, kissed her lightly on her forehead and wiped gently at her tears.

"Don't fret yourself, girl, I'm here now, you're going to be fine. I couldna' see you before … it's been nearly three days you've taken to come round properly." He checked the emotion in his voice. "Thank God, I say, you're alive."

"But what happened?" she was becoming exasperated. "Duncan, how did this …?

"You obviously canna' remember a thing, lass. Perhaps it's the best that way. Still, I forgive you for not turning up to meet me. Do you no' recall leaving the studios? You were supposed to be coming into town to meet me?" He tried to explain.

Sophie showed the vaguest signs of recollection.

"Well, you must have had a fiery scene with your boss man – Lionel?"

She tried to nod in agreement, but was too aware of pain in her neck and shoulders.

"The porter said your fairly ran out, not even bothering to acknowledge him as you usually do. You must have been totally preoccupied. You left your car in the car park and stomped off angrily. Outside the studio gates you had an altercation with a ten-ton truck! It mounted the pavement to avoid a woman with a pushchair. You had no chance by all accounts, but maybe if you'd not been so preoccupied – if you'd had your wits about you – you might have been able to take evasive action."

"If only I'd waited to let Lionel explain, I would have missed the whole thing …" she started.

"Exactly, just a chance accident, one of those millions-to-one things that always happens to someone else, in another town, eh?" he interrupted her.

"What day is it, Duncan?" she asked plaintively.

"It's Saturday, you've been here since Wednesday."

"How did you …?"

"That was easy – when you didna' arrive, I made enquiries. Lionel, that's your boss man, I take it, he filled me in. I've been coming every day to wait for you to wake up, ma sleeping beauty."

He smiled, leaned over and brushed straying hair from her face and kissed her forehead lightly.

"But you should be in Kenya by now," she remonstrated half-heartedly.

"Och no, I've had to make other arrangements. You'll be needing me around for a while. Broken legs, arms, all sorts of nasty contusions and the like that only a person in the trade can help you, you know!"

"But … you're a vet, not a doctor!"

"Your anatomy's not too complicated – I can adjust," he teased.

"And Kenya?" she queried.

"They've agreed to wait for me – besides, I might yet be able to convince you to join me for convalescence!

"Sounds very tempting, Duncan, certainly a better offer than I had at the studios the other day."

"You remember, then, what all the disagreement was? Lionel told me you'd thrown in your notice purely as an act of defiance, he said, something to do with that playwright chap – Markham. What's it all about?"

"Another time, Duncan, please. I'm so tired," she pleaded.

"Och, of course, ma dear girl," he agreed readily.

"I'll pop back later this evening and cheer you up a bit, eh?"

She attempted a smile as he turned to wave at the door.

When Sophie had had the telephone call from Lionel to meet him and discuss work on a new project, she had hardly expected to be confronted with Gregory Markham. Since the unexpected encounter at Chez Solange, Gregory had telephoned her flat four or five times and on each occasion her curtness and abrupt manner had ensured a swift end to the conversation. One evening he had rung and asked if he could call to see her and she tried to convince him she already had company.

"Not your Ginger Jock, again, is it?" he enquired with a trace of irritability.

Markham had been persistent, but Sophie had contrived to avoid his requests, doubting that she would be able to trust herself alone with him – such was the impact he could have on her. The chemistry between them was more than she could cope with and she was well aware that her fear of him stemmed from the fact that he was another woman's husband, and she had no intention of being his 'bit on the side'. She regretted the white lie and secretly urged Duncan to hurry back to the flat, for on this occasion Gregory was undeterred and despite Sophie's protestations had appeared at the flat half-an-hour later. To avoid a scene at the door, she had no alternative but to let him in.

"Why are you trying your damnedest to avoid me?" he asked bluntly.

Her fumbled denial did not satisfy him.

"You left the cottage in a rather shabby way, if I may say so – it was something of a shock and a disappointment to find you gone."

Without an invitation, he settled himself into the easy chair by the fire.

"The work was completed," she said hotly, "besides," she added, "I had other things to attend to in London."

"Like Ginger Jock, I suppose," he sneered.

"Will you not refer to Duncan in that unkind way, please," she said with a defensive tone in her voice.

His eyes rested on Duncan's pipe in the ash tray on the mantelshelf.

"Well, aren't you even going to offer me a coffee," he asked, "or do you save it all for Duncan?"

"I would have thought coffee would not be strong enough," she commented dryly.

"I only drink when I'm writing," he smiled, more amused than disconcerted.

She glanced at the clock to assure herself that Duncan's return was not too imminent. Half-an-hour, at least, she reflected, plenty of time to give him a coffee and have him gone long before Duncan arrives.

"Still not working, then, eh?" Gregory asked as she handed him coffee.

"What makes you say that?"

"An assumption on my part, I suppose."

"As a matter of fact, I'm not," she replied.

"I came to make you an offer," he said. His eyes pierced her and stilled her sharp retort before it reached her lips. "You needn't give me an answer now, I'll ring you tomorrow," he continued, placing his coffee cup on the small table at the side of his chair.

"I'm not in a position to take offers, Gregory," she said stiffly.

"Then what are you in a position for?" he demanded huskily. In one swift movement he leaped across, pulled her from her chair and drew her into his arms. With one arm holding her in a vice-like grip, his other hand curved her tender jaw and forced her face up towards him.

She gave a deep quivering sigh as she felt the throbbing impact of his lips on hers. He crushed her mouth roughly under his. She was conscious of pain.

His tongue forced open her trembling mouth, a hard, throbbing, pulsing pressure, as his hand slowly unbuttoned the top of her blouse and slid the silky material over her shoulder and she felt his lips pressing deeper and deeper into the soft muscle and then his tongue, moist and firm, caressing the skin. Suddenly she felt the sharp edge of his teeth as he ran the length of her shoulder teasing, tantalising until the pressure increased and a throb of ecstasy as his teeth bore more heavily and the conscious awareness of pain, hard and sweet, as the flesh was gently eased between his teeth, rhythmically, back and forth along the shoulder.

Then his lips, moist and tender, kissed along the bruised muscle. He moved his mouth to explore the soft hollow at the base of her throat and she was conscious of the dry tautness as she became more breathless with the sheer ecstasy of the moment. His lips brushed hers tenderly and he murmured, pushing aside the strap on her other shoulder, moving his mouth down carefully to slide his tongue with full pressure along the tender skin. Then his teeth probed for that most excitable erogenous area in the young muscle of her shoulder. She moaned with delight. His hand slid under her blouse and the warm, silky skin flinched before yielding to his touch. She eased herself into him and as his hands progressed sensuously over her breasts, his taut muscles pressed urgently against her slender body.

"Don't fight me, Sophie," he whispered thickly as his mouth brushed hers once more.

She couldn't resist the shameless craving as he expertly leaned her body backwards slowly into the couch and fell upon her with breathless excitement.
The telephone's shrill ring shocked her into reality.
Gregory quickly pulled himself from her.
Duncan's voice sounded far away.

"I'll not be getting back tonight, Sophie, would you believe it, we're fog-bound up here. No planes can take off."

"Where are you?" she asked shakily.

"Are you okay, girlie? You sound a bit strange – is everything alright?"

"Fine," she lied, normality returning to her voice, "where are you?"

"Aberdeen still! I've done all the finalising, seen my parents and so forth, but I canna get the flight back, not till tomorrow."
The pips sounded. "Och, I've no more change left, see you tomorrow." He was gone.

Sophie had never been more thankful for the telephone's ring.

"I think you'd better leave, Gregory," her voice was shaky as she moved behind the couch, momentarily out of his range. She wanted him desperately and had been on the brink of shattering all her principles, well aware that he could have had his own way completely. She sensed too that Gregory had been grateful for the interruption. Either that, or he was angry, for he left hurriedly with a brief apology, promising to ring on the following day. Sophie vowed to avoid him at all costs. He had the ability to manipulate her emotionally and physically and, not for the first time with Gregory, she felt totally exposed and vulnerable.

The following day she had had a call to meet Lionel at the studios.

The shock of seeing Gregory that afternoon in Lionel's office had shaken her reserve. His eyes had rested with ruthless interest on the full curves which her carefully fitting slacks and blouse had accentuated. It ought to have occurred to her before that Markham *must* have known Lionel Fairfax.

She cringed inwardly as she recalled how she had divulged all her feelings to Gregory and told him of the long conversation she had had with Lionel on the day she had arrived in Penzance all those weeks ago.

No wonder Markham had hinted about her not working when he had been at her flat two evenings previously. He had obviously put pressure to bear on Lionel in his insistence that Sophie be employed as a Production Assistant on his 'Man of Vision' drama. All her attempts to evade the contract failed and she realised she would inevitably be in close contact with Gregory since it was *his* script and he would be around the studios as he was planning to direct the production.

Even as she told Lionel she would rather give in

her notice than do the job, she added that her mind was half made up to go to Kenya with Duncan Armstrong. At the mere mention of that name, Gregory had shifted in his seat, visibly disturbed, and given her a threatening look which had quite unnerved her.

To go to Kenya would be the coward's way out, she realised that, but she thought she was being sensible in avoiding a married man and putting plenty of space and time between them. It would, she reasoned, ultimately help her to overcome the intense longing she felt for him. Although his calculating glances disturbed and unnerved her, she felt more than an odd excitement ripple through her when he touched her.

That afternoon, in Lionel's office, she flatly refused to be involved with the 'Man of Vision'. Many acrimonious things had been said. Markham had insisted that she knew the drama better than anyone since she had already worked on it for him. At that point, Lionel winked suggestively at Markham and Sophie's indignation was only roused further as she supposed Gregory to have divulged the sequence of events to Lionel and exposed her to further mortifying humiliation.

"If you don't accept it, then I'm afraid the script goes no further," Markham declared, an ominous ring to his voice.

"Well you're certainly not blackmailing *me* into anything," Sophie retorted furiously.

"Think about it, Sophie, and all the implications of turning down work in this business," Markham raked the fingers of one hand through his hair and gave an exaggerated sigh of weary resignation. With a sardonic expression, he added emphatically, "I'll ring you tonight."

"You needn't bother," she replied hotly over her shoulder. "And you will have my notice in writing tomorrow, Lionel," she added, storming out of the office.

A minute later she had been in the car park and realised she ought to burn some of her anger out before getting behind the wheel of a car.

She had hardly been aware of passing through the studio gates, not even conscious of which direction her feet were taking her.

Lying now, trussed up in plaster and slings, Sophie had plenty of time to recall that horrific moment. She had seen nothing, only now did she remember hearing a scream and a screeching of brakes, then a violent thud as a truck caught her, tossed her like a rag doll and then ... nothing.

All the effort of recall was too much for her now. She slept.

"Your mother telephoned, Miss Rayne. She's asked me to say she will be in this evening to see you," the Sister smiled as she took the thermometer from Sophie's mouth. "Hmm," she said significantly, marking the temperature on the board at the bottom of the bed. "And by the way, she'll have Henry with her," she added.

Sophie looked at the clock on the wall. Visitors were allowed in from seven until nine. Another three hours to lie waiting and thinking. She wondered if the "by the way" was a comment her mother had added or the Sister.

Sophie felt her mother sensed her disapproval of Henry, Gregory Markham's chauffeur-cum-general factotum. Three weeks earlier she had gone to the bungalow at Burnham Beeches.

"He's just a chauffeur, mother," she had remonstrated, and seeing the crushed look on her mother's face had immediately regretted the tactlessness.

Sophie had wanted to confide in her mother. There was so much to tell her. She was going through an emotional struggle over Gregory. He was already married and she wanted to ask her mother, "What do you do when you fall in love with another woman's husband?" and what do you do, she thought, when he makes it obvious he intends to have you! But Sophie realised that she was too far from her mother even to broach the subject, and seeing her so wrapped up in Henry she had decided to say nothing.

Major Henry Lingard, Gregory's 'man', as her mother referred to him, had been sent by his boss on a visit with flowers, especially for Mrs Rayne. A relationship had blossomed immediately and her mother was now living in another world. Sophie was happy for her.

But when she had broached the subject of her father's history notes, her mother had become very flustered and filled with apologies. She had had many chats with Mr Markham, and "knowing that he had been one of your father's students," she had said, "I simply could not resist letting him do something with them. After all, dear, he is already very famous, and I'm sure he'll do justice to your father's work."

Sophie had gone specifically to collect all of those old exercise books of her father's notes, intending to take up where her father had left off in 'The History of the English Village'. Since her

University days it had been one of her dreams to complete her father's work. And now Gregory had given all the books to Gregory Markham. Now it was too late! She would never be able to realise a dream for her father. It was a bitter blow for her to take.

On one occasion, when Gregory had telephoned her she had raised the subject of the village history notes and he offered to let her work with him. Sophie knew the price would be too high and declined.

Lying waiting, so helpless, she began to dread the evening visit and Henry, who, like Markham, had had such a profound impression on her mother.

Tall, self-assured, immaculately dressed in a dark grey suit, a rather sombre expression on a face that looked as if it had been polished into submission, he stood at the side of the bed and introduced himself.

"I wanted to meet you alone so that you could see me unclouded by your mother's warmth and attachment to me. I know much about you but you are clearly at a grave disadvantage in respect of myself."

She warmed to him. His eyes displayed the frank sincerity of his character and she sensed his attempt to cloak his nervousness with his short, matter-of-fact introduction, so short that she had not even had the opportunity to get a single word in!

"Henry, thank you for taking care of my mother. She needs someone like you – I'm very happy for both of you."

Henry relaxed immediately.

She smiled. "I'm sorry I can't offer you a hand, as you see, I'm trussed up like a turkey!"

He had anticipated opposition from Sophie, having been made aware of her closeness to her father, but they were laughing together as her mother arrived ten minutes later and the relief was written in Mrs Rayne's face as she tearfully leaned across the bed to her daughter.

Much later, Duncan joined them and his natural aptitude for hilarity ensured the meeting of all concerned went smoothly.

Henry and her mother had decided to marry during Easter and Sophie was delighted. It was proposed that Sophie move into the bungalow as soon as she could leave the hospital, rather than go back to a second-floor flat in the City.

When her visitors left, the nurse brought in flowers and chocolates. "You had another visitor, but he saw the family group around your bed and decided not to stay or interrupt." The card attached to the flowers read simply, "With my very deepest regards, Gregory."

As the nurse took her temperature half-an-hour later, she shook her head at the patient, "Too many visitors too soon, young lady, you are running at a fever pitch."

Sophie did not comment, knowing only too well what had caused her agitation since her visitors had left.

Every three days a bouquet of flowers arrived with a similar card attached. The writing on the card was no longer Gregory's scrawl and she assumed he was paying a secretary to deal with the formality of placating her with flowers to encourage her not to resign. After a couple of weeks there were simply so many flowers it was becoming an embarrassment and Sophie had to ask for them to be directed elsewhere. They unfortunately served as a constant reminder of *why* she was in hospital in the first place. And Sophie would have preferred to see the man rather than his floral tributes! Although she was only too well aware that seeing Gregory was by far the most dangerous thing to do, considering her weak state emotionally and physically and her total vulnerability.

Lying day after day, scarcely able to move, she had far too much time to dally with the idle thoughts of being seduced by another woman's husband. And she had also to reconsider her future when she 'was' out of hospital. Her threat to Lionel Fairfax was real still in her mind, because she knew only too well she could not be around Gregory Markham. Fearful enough of his physical influence over her, Sophie did not want to put herself into such a compromising situation, for she was afraid also of her own attraction to him. It went deeper even than a sexual, physical magnetism towards him. On an intellectual level, she found him stimulating and that could be dangerous for her inasmuch as it would open the door to heart and body.

After three weeks, she had seen little of anyone but her mother and of course … Duncan. He had been given his ultimatum for Kenya and had less than three months or forfeit the post. Sophie was so indebted to him for delaying his departure on her account but sensed too that he hoped she would go with him to Kenya if he proved himself indispensable to her.

She explained as much to her mother one afternoon, but deliberately omitted to reveal all her other misgivings, particularly in relation to Gregory Markham.

Her mother, though, was now totally

preoccupied with her wedding and future with Henry and told Sophie that after the wedding she and Henry would be leaving on a world tour. She had a faraway look in her eyes.

Sophie, not wishing to dampen her mother's enthusiasm, casually mentioned finance.

"Henry's in control of that dear – he's very well placed," she added, also that he would be leaving Gregory's employ.

"Oh, and by the way …," she coloured and moved over to look out of the window into the hospital grounds.

"By the way what?" Sophie asked, when it seemed as if her mother had forgotten what to say next.

"The cottage …"

"What about it, mother?"

"Well, I … I've sold it," her voice was unsteady and she turned round briefly with a look of resignation.

"Oh, mother, no! You can't have!"

"I haven't been for so long now, and you know it holds too many memories for me to … to… I didn't want to go again, not with Henry. We're starting a new life, now."

"You never said! You've just gone and done without ever asking me? Mother, I'd have paid you for it!" Sophie was crying with exasperation and despair. Her mother's sense of timing left much to be desired. The utter disappointment filled her with desolation and she felt the last blow had been dealt to cripple her for good.

Her mother was genuinely surprised to see the effect her statement had had on her daughter.

"I never thought you'd bother … please, come on now, Sophie, I didn't think you'd such an attachment to the old place."

"Of course I have. You know I went down in January, didn't you? It's my haven from … from … from all of this," she sobbed, gesturing hopelessly with a sweep of her plastered arm.

"But you can still go, dear, he'll let *you* go, I'm sure," her mother tried consoling her.

"Who will?"

"Why, Gregory. He's bought it. He paid me cash!"

Sophie's heart sank.

Long after her mother had left, Sophie was struggling to quell her anger with her mother's crassitude. Something had gone seriously wrong with their relationship. She blamed herself, working away, living away for such long stretches, she had lost touch with her mother's confidences. They had grown apart. Since her mother had met Gregory Markham, there had been a distinct change.

She had let the cottage to him, handed over all of her husband's history notebooks, a lifetime of his work, and now she had sold the cottage to him. Goodness knows what else he had manipulated her into doing. It didn't bear thinking about, Sophie decided. Stuck in a hospital bed she could do nothing. She wanted to telephone Markham and give him a piece of her mind but she couldn't even hold a 'phone. Besides, according to her mother, Henry had taken Gregory to Heathrow Airport for a flight to America.

Sophie had tried to appear indifferent when her mother had babbled on about him, how he had sold the rights to two plays and they were making a film.

He would be in America for two or three months. He wouldn't even be back for the wedding, although he had insisted that Henry hold the reception at the Elizabethan Manor in Surrey, which Gregory called 'home'.

"He's paying for the reception, too, as a wedding present," her mother had said. "He was most emphatic about that!" she had added.

Sophie, who normally relished solitude, was becoming increasingly depressed, with such restricted movement because of her injuries, and trapped in a private side ward. For the first three weeks, she had been compelled to lie still within the confines of a plaster jacket and encased legs, unable even to indulge herself with a book to read. The studio had organised a video and a large supply of film, but she was unable to operate it without assistance.

Lionel Fairfax had been an early visitor, feeling responsible in some way for her situation. Lying flat on her back, she had never seen Lionel from such an angle before and there was something slightly ridiculous about this great bull of a man, sallow, exceptionally broad and running to fat, as he padded around her bed with a solicitous manner which bordered on obsequiousness. He deliberately did not mention the controversial topic of 'A Man of Vision' and only touched on work when he reassured her that, for the purposes of ensuring her sick benefits would not be affected, he had ignored her threat of notice and retained her on full salary.

One morning, she asked the Sister if she could be moved to a general ward.

"Oh, no, Miss Rayne," was the starchy reply, "this was all paid for privately *and* in advance. You're to have every convenience – besides, it would never do to have you on a general ward, it would be so unfair to the other patients."

"But I'm not paying privately," came the exasperated reply, "I simply don't have that kind of money."

"Someone does, obviously!" the Sister declared as she left, not prepared to discuss the matter any further.

"Duncan," Sophie declared later that day, you're very sweet, paying for my hospitalisation like this – but I'd rather not be a private patient, if you don't mind."

"You're thanking the wrong person, girlie," Duncan asserted, "I've done no such knightly act. Maybe the studios are paying?"

"Hardly! I thought it *must* be you. It certainly can't be mother – although she could have used the proceeds from the sale of the cottage. I really must find out. It's quite ridiculous paying like this."

"Och, don't worry about it, you'll be out next week, anyway!"

She sighed. Hospitalisation was depressing enough, but a huge chunk of her life had been simply wasted lying in the hospital bed – so much she was missing, never to be recaptured. She couldn't wait to get home!

Duncan's daily visits had been the bright spot in her boredom of hospitalisation. She was only too conscious of the kind consideration he had given to her, and that he had quietly, but persistently, been 'working' on Sophie and that each day he felt he had won her over a little more. He hoped to take her with him. If he had to leave without her with only promises that she would follow him, her would lose her. As it was, he had deliberately made himself indispensable.

With so much time on her own to think, she weighed all the advantages in settling to go with Duncan. The only point in its disfavour, she realised, was the fact that she did not love him. Her feelings lacked passion and the strong, heady moments of physical need. She reassured herself that a healthy relationship didn't necessarily require those ingredients. She refused to believe that she was deluding herself when she remembered the sensations which Gregory had roused in her. She could exercise control and subjugate her emotions, if necessary. Besides, her attitude towards Gregory now was one of grave hostility.

He had wormed his way into her mother's affections and inveigled her into parting with the history notes and then the cottage. She realised that if she had not gone to the cottage in January she would never have met him. But he would *still* have exerted his influence on the Rayne family, even though she would not have come into contact with him over 'A Man of Vision', because Lionel could take his pick from the studio for Production Assistants.

Gregory could not have claimed the precedent that she was already familiar with the work. All in all, she would not have been lying in hospital now, held together in plaster casts! She held Gregory responsible for all the current dissonance in her life and her aversion towards him was exacerbated even further when the Sister later informed her that Mr

Gregory Markham was footing the bill for the hospital treatment. Despite her repugnance at the idea of his financial assistance, she reflected that it was probably a just retribution for taking so much from her in other ways – her father's notes and the cottage, not to mention her peace of mind!

Perhaps it was guilt on his part. She decided not to let Duncan know the name of her benefactor.

Two weeks before Easter she had the plaster removed from her neck and arm and one of the leg plasters and began twice daily physiotherapy sessions. The doctor, Mincing by name and by nature, Sophie thought, was pleased with her progress. Slowly she began to move around on crutches, but only for very short periods. Dr Mincing, despite his earlier promise to send her home, had kept her in. It had been a bitter blow to Sophie, but she accepted his judgement when she realised just how much of a burden she would be at the bungalow, still incapacitated, wheelchair-bound or on crutches. With her mother's wedding so imminent, she was much better out of the way.

Inevitably, she saw less of her mother in the days leading up to Easter and although she had been kept informed of all the arrangements, when Duncan took her out to the bungalow, two days before Good Friday, she felt like an intruder. She had had no opportunity to share her mother's excitement of preparation and planning and it only caused her to feel more isolated and withdrawn from mother.

The prolonged period in hospital had left her with a sense of detachment and depression.

# CHAPTER 8

The ceremony had been a brief and very private affair at the Registrar's Office in London. The guests were few – Henry's brother, unmistakably a smaller and younger version of the bridegroom, Sophie's spinster aunt who muttered words of disapprobation throughout, Duncan and Sophie. It had been arranged that way by Henry, who for all his outward show of confidence was a man easily embarrassed by ceremonials. The reception was to be another matter. Markham's Rolls had been provided for the drive into Surrey for the wedding reception.

Robin Markham had arrived promptly to act as chauffeur to the couple, and Duncan, who had been given explicit instructions on the whereabouts of the Markham mansion, followed discreetly in a hired car.
Sophie's one leg was still in plaster and throughout the ceremony she had been in a wheelchair. She had crutches, but found it exceedingly tiring for any length of time to support herself on them. Duncan had thoughtfully hired a large, roomy estate car to take the wheelchair and at the same time give plenty of room for her outstretched left leg.

Once the car left London, Sophie found herself inclined to doze. The hectic life of the previous two days had been in sharp contrast to the tedium of her weeks in hospital. About an hour later, Duncan squeezed her hand gently to wake her up.

"Grandeur, ma dear girl, welcome to the playwright's modest abode!" he mocked, turning the car through the huge iron gates under the towered gatehouse. He drove slowly along an avenue of ash and beech which tapered into shrubberies on either side of the gravel drive, winding through formal gardens, past a large lake with a poplared island that resembled a becalmed ship, and sweeping majestically right to the front of the house. Sophie had to confess to Duncan that she felt awed and was compelled to ask herself what on earth could have driven Markham to rent, and now indeed buy, her mother's very modest Cornish cottage.

"Can't imagine why he needed your mother's place, lassie," Duncan echoed her thoughts, "what a property!"

Eighteenth century classical façades masked the extensive remains of a large Tudor mansion that was now an attractive agglomeration of grey stone with a battlemented tower and late Gothic windows. Barton Manor had a beauty and quiet dignity to its exterior that promised an exciting plethora of intriguing, dramatic and historic and anecdotal revelations to any visitor. But Sophie's love of the past guaranteed that, whatever else happened, she would be totally captivated by the aura of such a building. She was speechless.

Robin Markham, a pale, shadowy copy of his father, had arrived ahead of them and helped Duncan with Sophie's wheelchair. Duncan carried her up the entrance steps and helped her into the chair. She felt awkward and frustrated having to rely on assistance. She longed to explore the building with its sumptuous galleries, drawing rooms, elaborate decoration, quiet wainscotted rooms, narrow passages, twisting staircases and the inevitable, fascinating confusion of kitchens, cellars and turret rooms.

"Everyone's congregated in the Dining Room," Robin said, "but I expect you'd like the powder room first, Sophie, so I'll call Sarah to assist you." She nodded her assent but Robin had already gone for his sister.

Sarah, petite and girlish, despite her sixteen years, met Sophie with a warm grin of approval and took her into a cloakroom under the expansive oak staircase.

"Henry is so fortunate to meet someone like your mother," Sarah bubbled excitedly.

"You've met her then?"

"Oh yes, many times. Henry has often brought her down here on his days off, but of course when he's driven us anywhere, your mother has sometimes come along for the ride, so to speak. As Daddy says, he'll be in very caring hands with your mother."

A lump came to Sophie's throat to think that Gregory had spoken of her mother in that vein, but at the same time a pang of jealousy shot through her. Her mother had never once mentioned that she had been to Barton Manor, nor had she spoken of Gregory's children. She felt decidedly uncomfortable and at a disadvantage. Her non-committal replies must have been something of a disappointment to Sarah, although she did not display any sign of it as she wheeled Sophie into the splendid Dining Room that was more like a State Room!

It contained a large collection of family pictures ranged around the walls, rare furniture, rugs and tapestries, but had as a centrepiece an enormous

Jacobean table laid out with a magnificent wedding feast. Her mother was standing at the far end of the room with Henry, admiring the gardens beyond. Duncan came across to meet her.

"It's a champagne toast to your mother, Sophie," he handed her a glass. "And your playwright friend's here!" he added dryly.

Sophie had thought he was in America. He walked directly towards her as Duncan moved to the table for more champagne.

"And how's the invalid?" Gregory asked gently.

"Mending nicely, thank you," came the limp reply. She was smarting with annoyance at Gregory for two or three reasons, not the least being the payment of the hospital bill. She would not give him the satisfaction of thinking she had any interest in him by questioning his return from America.

"You're still with Ginger Jock, I see?"

"Do you have to be so insulting? Duncan is very close to me and I resent your attitude towards him – it's quite unjustified as far as I'm concerned," she snapped.

"I thought he was off to minister to sick animals – have you persuaded him against it?"

"Quite the reverse, actually, it's just a question of getting me out of plaster."

"Then what? You're surely not intending to go with him?" His face hardened and he spoke through clenched teeth. He bent towards her and whispered angrily, "there'll be me to reckon with if your do so much as dare to think about going to Kenya."

"And since when have you been my keeper? Just because you paid the hospital bills it doesn't entitle you to make my decisions."

His expression was grim, and she immediately regretted mentioning the money.

"Don't you dare ruin your mother's day!" His voice was taut with anger, his mouth curved in an unkind smile.

She was grateful for Duncan's return, but Gregory moved off instantly without acknowledging him.

"He looks like a man containing anger," Duncan remarked, "What have you said to upset him?" he grinned, little realising the truth of his observation.

The room began to fill now with guests and Henry with his new bride moved amongst them making all the necessary gestures and thanks. A large number of the guests were Henry's army colleagues from days past. A few of the Markham family were there, including Mrs Markham, who had deigned to put in an appearance and had nodded to Sophie from across the room but made no attempt to mingle with anyone.

"At last, Sophie," her mother's hand touched her shoulder, "there are so many people – I scarcely know them all and they all look so extravagant!"

"But you look delightful, mother, and that's a far more worthy state to be in," she reassured her. "I must say that you have a wonderful aura of happiness around you – you are both so splendid together."

"Thank you, dear. Henry's so dependable. I feel as if I have a strong support to lean on – I've not had that since ... for so long." She swallowed with emotion. "You *do* like Henry, don't you, dear, only you did say he was only a ..."

"I know what I once said in a moment of angry hurt when I had not even met him – and I very quickly changed my opinion. He's first-class, but then so are you," she responded warmly to her mother.

She clutched at Sophie's hand and bent to kiss her. "I'm so happy, and I only hope that you will let someone do the same for you, dear. And don't be angry with Gregory – I get the impression that you don't like him. He's a good man. It was so kind of him to lay on all of this for us – and he flew back from America, just to be here today. He's surprised all of us."

You can say that again, Sophie thought inwardly, and would have liked to add her side of Gregory to the picture, but had no intention of shattering her mother's illusions about him.

"Quite a mansion he has, isn't it?" she said obliquely.

"Mm, yes," her mother seemed rather disinterested by the opulence of it all.

"Have you had a guided tour?" Sophie tried to draw her mother a little.

"Gregory has taken me round. *You'll* like it dear, so much history here, and so many rooms."

"I can't think what he needed with our humble little Cornish retreat, mother," she eyed her intently as she spoke.

"I'm sure you'll find that Gregory has his reasons, he usually does," she replied shrewdly, "but I don't want you to bring that up just now, dear," she reddened, "I'd rather not discuss that part of my life anymore. Gregory will explain everything to you."

"But *I'm* part of your old life, mother," Sophie persisted, just realising what had *really* happened to her mother as she had tried to cloak all past emotions and events to face a totally new future with an entirely different type of man. She was not sure it was a healthy thing to do and she wondered ruefully how much was suggestion and influence from Henry.

"Now let me fetch something from the buffet for you," her mother either had not heard her plea or chose to ignore it. There were certain subjects, Sophie realised, that her mother would simply not discuss.

Duncan returned with a silver tray and had chosen a tasty sample of the large variety of dishes from the table.

"Mother's gone to do the same thing," she said, "I'll be like the side of a bus – don't forget I've had no exercise for weeks!"

"A little extra weight will improve you! No, actually she saw me first and I told her not to bother. Besides, you could run it off in Kenya." "Can I rely on you to come, Sophie?"

"Duncan," she took his hand and squeezed it fondly, "Duncan, you've been a pillar of strength to me, but let me make the decision when I'm capable of it. I'm too vulnerable in this contraption."

"I understand, don't fret. You'll come if you really want to, I know that."

There were times when she wished Duncan were not quite so understanding. Stolid and reliable, those were his good qualities, but she had hoped more than once for a fiery streak of passion to burst forth and dominate her. She had to admit that, despite her protestations to the contrary, she could appreciate physical domination. Sophie knew she could have that with Gregory – but the price was too high. She would never be a man's mistress.

Gregory was standing talking to Henry and her mother. She looked at the broad back that was turned towards her, the dark hair curling low into his neck, overlapping the collar of his cream silk shirt, the width of his shoulders, the tapering towards his waist and the lean, muscular hips. The desire to touch him gave her physical pain, but she had to fight the insanity of her own contemplations.

Gregory turned unexpectedly as if by thought transference, and caught her eye. He could convey and impression of intimacy with a look. A shiver went down her spine. There was a ruthless intention as he held her eyes, demanding response. Briefly, his tongue etched the outline of his upper lip in an alarmingly sensuous movement. She swallowed involuntarily and brought her hand up to her own mouth to hide the trembling lower lip.

At that moment, Mrs Markham joined their trio and it was obvious from their actions that she was about to leave the party. Strange, Sophie thought, perhaps she has an engagement elsewhere.

On the pretext of wanting the cloakroom, Sophie manoeuvred herself in the wheelchair out of the Dining Room, declining help from Duncan. Once out of sight of the entrance to the room, she steered her chair towards the long, oak-panelled corridor leading to the rear of the house.

A door on her left was ajar and without too much difficulty she wheeled herself into an expansive room filled with tapestries, oil painting portraits and furniture in the Georgian and Louis Sixteenth style. Sophie was quite breathless. She steered herself out again into the corridor at the end of which she found the Library, smaller than the Drawing Room she had just left, but warmer and friendlier.

She gazed spellbound at the hundreds of books, a fine collection of rare and valuable volumes. She ran her fingers across the leather spines of some of the books not covered in by glass. More oil portraits lined the walls, and she moved to the marble fireplace, drawn by the huge portrait of a very familiar face. The inscription underneath caused her to flush hotly. 'Sir Gregory Markham-Spender'.

It was all too much to take in. Sophie had had no idea of his title, and looking slowly around at the other portraits she could have kicked herself for not seeing a family likeness. No wonder he thought he could rule people's lives, she surmised angrily. It's obviously in the blood – and a long line of Markham-Spenders glared down at her censoriously from all around the Library.

He had *all this* – and it was *still* not enough. He had to possess even their humble little Cornish cottage. For a long time the cottage had been a very private haven, a place to run when the world crowded in and when she wanted to find freedom. There had always been a magic in the very name of the county, and despite the hundreds of visits to the cottage, it had lost none of its aura. She loved it in all of its moods, but especially its cold, damp, misty mood.

Sophie actually enjoyed the cold, damp, grey Cornish mist. It suited her character admirably, for at times she was only too aware there was an incomprehensible void in her life. She relished the quiet, lonely moments and realised at times that it was morbid to indulge in her solitary company so much. It was something her colleagues could never quite fathom out in her. She enjoyed long, lonely hours and counted them precious.

Cornwall for Sophie abounded in history, atmosphere and mystery and she admired the stubborn pride of the Cornish character and their reluctance to accept strangers too readily. Descended from a people pushed back into the south-westerly tip of the island by invaders, the Celtic spirit seemed to smoulder still within them, ever-ready to ignite, and their fiery independence admitted nothing and no-one too willingly.

She had spent many of her formative years in Cornwall and the influence of the Cornish had not been wasted on her. She felt she was going home when she went to the cottage, for the rugged beauty and the mystery always beckoned her. As soon as she had crossed the Tamar River that cut the County off from the rest of England, she would feel on home territory and sensed that relief which the traveller feels, having roamed willingly, but always grateful to return.

A very strong resentment had welled up insider her. It seemed as if his wealth gave him the authority to treat everyone else with contempt. He was buying pleasures but at the expense of anyone who happened to cross his path. Duncan had experienced the same kind of behaviour with Vanessa's family. An exaggerated flamboyance with money that totally disregarded people and their feelings. A self-satisfied hauteur which seemed to them to acknowledge their own superiority.

No wonder she felt such understanding over what had happened to Duncan. He had only been half right when he said that too much money borders on the obscene – it isn't the money that is the problem, it is the licence and liberty which it accords to its possessor, she reflected. It galled her to think that he had openly had the audacity to pay for the hospital bills and she had already decided to return his money when she was fully mobile again, not wishing to be beholden to him in any way.

She moved the chair to the window bay which overlooked the gardens, filled with rare conifers and shrubs, including hydrangeas, magnolias, rhododendrons, camellias and roses. Beyond, on the rise, lay surrounding land, covered with gorse and bracken and a belt of wild woodland. She assumed that the whole encompassed the hundreds of acres of Barton manor.

"Ever seeking solitude," Gregory's voice surprised her. She had not closed the door on entering and he had made no noise crossing the carpeted floor.

"I hope I didn't presume too much upon your hospitality in wandering at will around your home," she said caustically.

"My pleasure. In fact, I'm delighted that you are taking an interest."

"Oh, one likes to see how the other half lives from time to time, Sir Gregory," was her terse reply.
His mouth quirked. So, you've realised. I wondered how long before you'd hold that against me," he smiled, then, more amused than disconcerted.

"I'm sure you had some motive," she said stiffly, "deceit comes naturally to you, obviously."

"Actually, you're quite wrong, Sophie," he amended coolly, "I've had no intention of deceiving anyone. It's simply more expedient to stick to the plain old Markham name."

"How nice to have the choice," she said archly, tossing her head to signify disinterest.

"Never a truer word spoken," he agreed, "titles,

hereditary or otherwise, Sophie, can be a burden. It was a long time ago that I dropped the Spender name – when I was at Oxford to be precise. Titles were ten-a-penny, anyway, and I decided I preferred people to accept me for what I was capable of rather than what heredity had furnished me with. Quite contrary to what you think about me, I needed my writing to be *accepted* not *bought* by a title."

"Frankly, I couldn't care less," she said coldly, "you and people like you can always offer that as an excuse – but should you have failed simply as Markham, I don't doubt for one minute that you would have used your title to gain privileges."

"Sophie, don't hold my title against me," he flashed angrily, "I didn't buy it, for God's sake – I inherited it. At times it's been like a millstone. What do you think the upkeep is on this place alone?"

"Really, I'm not interested. But if it is such a financial burden, why add to it by furnishing yourself with other properties?" Her voice was savage.

"You've found out then?"

"Only by accident – if you'll pardon the pun! And it leads me onto another matter – all that money you lavished on my hospital bills – I intend to repay you as soon as I'm mobile. I don't want your charity!" she snapped.

"You're very ungracious – but I think that under the present circumstances, and not being in possession of all the facts, you are justified in feeling as you do. In some small way, I held myself responsible for that accident. If I hadn't insisted so vehemently to Lionel, the meeting would have been concluded more amicably," he apologised.

"Don't you believe it," she declared, "you can't

buy me, Sir Gregory," she said scornfully.

"Oh, my dear love, I don't intend to," he said, an ominous ring in his voice as he sharply spun her chair towards him, the desperate look of a hungry predator in his eyes. He pressed his hands down on her shoulders, the strength of his fingers biting into her tender flesh.

She flinched.

"I don't intend to *buy* you," he insisted, his face so close to hers and the deep, penetrating eyes stilled her.

Her throat tightened.

"I think we both know that I *can* and *will* have you. It is simply a question of time." His eyes glittered derisively now.

The dryness in her mouth prevented her from making any retort and she only gave a little gasp as he touched the outline of her mouth with his forefinger and then pressed his finger back on his own lips.

"I won't take advantage of you now," he murmured, "but oh, my Sophie, you are so very ... vulnerable," his voice had softened and purred at her hypnotically.

Her face, a haunted white with both excitement and anger, she stared at him, feeling his incensed breath scorching her cheeks. The male scent of him invaded her nostrils and her heart began to beat unevenly.

He brought his mouth down swiftly on hers and there was no pretence in the trembling mouth which parted naturally and willingly under the pressure of his.

"I *shall* have you, Sophie," her murmured with quiet assurance, as he drew slowly from her.

She shivered, half with excitement, half fear.

"Am I interrupting a private party?" Duncan's voice broke across the room.

It was late evening when Duncan drew up the car outside the bungalow back at Burnham Beeches. Sophie felt decidedly weary, more from the emotional tension of the day than from anything physical. The atmosphere between them had been strained, both of them attempting to pretend that the incident in the Library at Barton Manor had not taken place.

Sophie could not be sure how long Duncan had been standing there and what he had seen and heard before he had interrupted them. She had hesitated to broach the subject, waiting for Duncan's lead, if there was to be one, so that she could judge from his comments the extent of what he knew.

Gregory had preferred some feeble comment about kissing the bride's next of kin being second best. As usual, his rapier mind, with quick and incisive wit had saved them all from a potentially embarrassing scene. He had left her alone with Duncan and she was quick to point out the portrait over the marble fireplace.

"Och," he noted disparagingly, "I might have known there was a whiff of aristocracy somewhere – the smell is familiar to me! I'm not too impressed wi' the man's manners, actually," he added with disdain.

"He didn't bring me in here," she replied, defending Gregory.

"Och, I know," he agreed, "but I saw him watching you leaving the Dining Room and he followed you all right. There's more to that man than meets the eye – I can tell you."

"How do you mean?" Sophie reddened, wondering just what and how much Duncan *did* know.

"Och, look, I wasn't going to tell you this, but … oh, never mind … I've no claim on you, I know that, I'm just a man living in hope, that's all."

"What were you about to tell me?"

"The day you asked me about paying your hospital bill, well, I checked up on the way out with Sister. I wasn't going to tell you – but then I …" he tailed off.

"It's all right, Duncan," she interrupted, "I know it's Markham, or rather Markham-Spender! I found out from the Sister too. Don't worry, I intend to repay him in full as soon as I'm able to get to a bank."

"That's a relief! I was beginning to assume that he was taking more than a paternalistic interest in you." His expression grew faintly sardonic.

"He wouldn't get far if he did," Sophie felt the lie within her, knowing full well Gregory's capabilities and his final veiled threat still ringing in her ears.

No more had been said and they had joined the other guests back in the Dining Room. Gregory gave no hint of what had taken place and virtually ignored her for the rest of the afternoon. The bride and groom left for Heathrow Airport and the party broke up.

Gregory disappeared at the same time as her mother and Henry and it was only later she found out from Robin that he was taking a flight himself.

"Quite an extravagance, I'd say, Duncan had snorted. "No disrespect to the wedded pair, of course, but it's odd that he should fly back just for the wedding. His wife cleared off pretty sharply, too, did you notice?"

Sophie was reminded of the time Penelope Markham had come all the way to Cornwall in January to find her husband out.

"They certainly don't appear to co-ordinate their movements too well," she commented wryly.

Going into the bungalow alone with Duncan gave her a peculiar sense of being an intruder. The bungalow was her mother's home and had her unmistakable mark upon it – so to enter when she was away inevitably gave rise to strange feelings within her. It differed from going into a hotel, because of their very anonymity. The spare room had been made ready for Duncan, and Sophie was grateful for his company.

"I don't think I could have come here on my own, Duncan," she quietly commented to him later that evening, "somehow it would have felt as if I had lost my mother completely coming to the empty bungalow alone."

"You know, Sophie," Duncan slipped his arm around her as she sat on the settee. "You don't have to be alone. The choice is yours. I can't make myself any plainer to you." He looked at her keenly.
Sophie interpreted his meaning.

"Duncan, I promise I'll give you an answer soon."

"When? You know I shan't be able to keep holding my job open indefinitely. I have to be away soon – besides, it's so long since I practised my art, I'll have forgotten what veterinary surgery is all about," he tried to make light of a serious situation.

"I promise to let you know the day after the

plaster is off my leg."

"One week, then? Okay. It's a deal, but remember what I said about living accommodation. We'd have to be living as man and wife."

"But I realise that, of course, I wouldn't come at all if it wasn't the whole works!"

"In that case, I'll keep my fingers crossed for just that," he returned swiftly.

That night, Sophie slept fitfully. Although her reason acknowledged that it would be wrong to capitulate to Gregory, she had an irrepressible urge to abandon herself to the passion he roused in her. And that is exactly what it would be in real terms – an abandonment, for it was not a relationship which could ever amount to anything more than an affair while Gregory had a wife. To sacrifice a reputation and become a married man's mistress for the sake of moments of passion, lose self-respect – no, it was too high a price to pay.

The alternative was Duncan, safe and reliable, loving, warm and sensitive, but without passion. Maybe that side of the relationship would be unnecessary and satisfaction could be derived from work and being in another environment.

Sometime during the half-waking, half-sleeping state she counselled herself on the other obvious alternative. She could decide to continue in her job as before, refuse Duncan's offer, *and* avoid Gregory. In reminding herself of his persistence, like a terrier that has something in its grip and will not let go, she came to the conclusion that the latter option would not be feasible. Gregory's manner did not brook disobedience and she knew that, despite her resentment and indignation over the history notes, the purchase of the cherished cottage and his attitude over the hospital bill, she *still* wanted him. She argued with herself that it could not be love and the idea that she physically needed him left her with a feeling of abhorrence. That made her no better than Mitch Peters. It would be weakness to succumb to mere physical satisfaction.

For the next few days Duncan avoided even mentioning Kenya.

She had become more adept now at shifting herself about with the aid of crutches and they had daily visits back to the hospital for physiotherapy on her neck, arms and leg.

At the end of the week, Duncan drove her to the flat and she waited downstairs in the car whilst he collected a long list of items she had written down. He also brought what post had accumulated in her short sojourn at the bungalow.

"Here, looks as if this is from your boss man!" Duncan handed her a letter with the studio's franked postmark on it. He watched her expectantly while she read. Sophie cleverly hid her surprise at the content of the letter and brushed it off lightly when Duncan raised the subject on the way back to Burnham Beeches.

While she was alone later that afternoon she took the letter out again and read it a second time. It was most providential! Lionel's offer let her off the hook completely. And she knew she would have no hesitation in accepting the choice contract he was offering her. All those nights she had tossed and turned trying to come to a decision over Duncan or Gregory! Now the only real viable option had been presented to her.

She rang Lionel for more details while Duncan was away in the City the following morning.

"Of course I'm serious," Lionel convinced her, "but you'll have to be fit for this one."

"I shall be," she assured him. "I'll be fully ready in just over a week."

"You'd better be, Sophie, a lot of wrangling and competition has been caused over this job."

"I appreciate it," she said sincerely, "you'll never know how much. Thanks for thinking about me."

"I think we *all* owe you one, darling," he added cryptically. Before Duncan returned, Sophie began to assemble her thoughts on how best to divulge everything to him. It would be unfair to wait, it only delayed hurting him. Besides, it would enable her to begin preparations for her own contract.

"The way I see it," Duncan admitted when she had explained about her job, "you haven't really said 'No' to me, you've actually said 'Yes' to a damned interesting contract."

"Thank you for seeing it that way, I wouldn't want to miss this for anything. I've never been to Hong Kong and I don't suppose I'll ever have the chance again."

"Actually, it mitigates my disappointment – over these last few days I've thought that you were going to give me the bird over that fellow Markham," he said with relief.

"Whatever gave you that impression?" she asked, colour rushing to her face.

"The man's crazy for you – it takes nothing to see that. The night we met in Chez Solange he couldn't take his eyes off you. Even his wife must have sensed that."

"Oh, Duncan, don't be absurd," she laughed, "he's just a flirtatious philanderer."

"Exactly, that's what's worried me. Tell me, has he ever made a pass at you?"

"Really, Duncan! her eyes widened. Do you think I couldn't handle myself if he did? She begged the question.

"From that, I take it that he *has*," his voice had an air of resignation.

"Duncan, he's married!"

"He's also very persuasive."

"That doesn't say very much for me, though, does it?"

"I didn't mean it to sound as if you're loose, I know damned well you're not. Truth is, I'm probably a wee bit jealous," he admitted.

"Well, you needn't be," she reassured him, feeling exceedingly guilty as she knew he was right.

"Chaps like that seem to draw a woman like a magnet. Romancing comes very easy to them. I've never been able to be that licentious. Perhaps I've missed out on something, eh?"

"You're fine the way you are. The sort of man a woman can rely on, know he'll always be there, safe, solid and enduring in a relationship."

"But still you won't come with me to Kenya," he said gloomily, "or can I hope that after Hong Kong you'll give up the life you lead to become a Vet's assistant?"

"Let's take it as it comes, who knows, in a matter of weeks you'll be so wrapped up in your work you'll forget I ever existed."

"An extremely unlikely prospect. Still, I'm grateful for the pleasures I've had these past few weeks. We'll be friends, Sophie, whatever happens, eh?"

She nodded, relieved that he had taken everything so well.

# CHAPTER 9

It seemed to Sophie that Fate had been working against her and almost totally defeated her.

With no reason given, the Hong Kong documentary was shelved just days before the TV crew were about to depart, and when Brad Merrill, the producer, was commiserating with her, he half-hinted that it might never happen now anyway.

It was a shattering blow to Sophie because Hong Kong had been her hope of getting away from so many recent traumas – not the least being Gregory Markham.

Seven weeks, with so much distance between her and the one man who had had so much influence on her life in the last few months, directly and indirectly, would have given her the opportunity of re-building her shattered emotions. Her life had turned upside down in six months and nothing ever promised to be the same again.

Some of her confidence and trust in other people had been destroyed over the Mitch Peters incident and then she had suddenly found herself thrust into a decidedly weird situation in Cornwall and realised, since, how attracted she was to Markham. Her mother had gone through an almost total metamorphosis and the calm, quiet reassurance of her nature was no longer available. The cottage in Cornwall, a 'safe refuge', had been sold out of her reach. The accident had given her a lot of time to reflect on the emptiness of her existence apart from her work, and even now, her work had just been taken away from her without proper explanations. Hong Kong had definitely promised to be a way of re-inspiring her after so much unhappiness and trauma over the last months.

Reluctantly, she accepted an invitation to have lunch with Lionel Fairfax and Gregory Markham to discuss a new contract, knowing full well what they had in mind.

In her current situation, she didn't seem to have much choice.

"Let's see if we can make it a more amicable meeting than the last time," Lionel urged.

Sophie had needed no reminding – her wounds had healed but there were plenty of scars, and a slight limp in her left leg. The only good thing about *that*, she reflected, had been the fact that she *had* survived the altercation with the truck.

At the last moment, Gregory had sent his apologies and Sophie had been relieved and disappointed. She had not seen him since her mother's wedding at Easter, but she had felt his influence and dominance over her life and she had not relished the inevitable confrontation with him. Maybe he had planned it that way, thinking that perhaps the whole event might go more smoothly if he were not present. On the other hand, she decided, he was too much of an egoist to miss the opportunity of scoring over her.

It was over lunch, however, when she had signed

her contract, that Lionel disclosed the extent of Gregory's influence.

"We're *all* in his pay," he said with resignation, "so you needn't feel as if you've 'given in'. He owns a large share in the Company."

"I don't believe it," she started, "but then, yes, I suppose I *can* see it – he does appear to be a man who must possess all or nothing," she finished scathingly.

"Not quite a definition of him, darling," Lionel asserted, "but it's not for me to persuade you otherwise."

Sophie had become a little more cautious in her dealings with anyone remotely connected to Gregory. Only too aware of his influence and power, and the fact that he appeared to have control over so many people, she waited for Lionel to continue.

"I don't think I've *ever* encountered such a determined man, Sophie – he certainly wants *you*!" Lionel declared.

"Well, he's got me now – but promise me, Lionel, no more entanglements, please – I'm only taking *this* contract to make life easier for a lot of other people."

"That's not quite what I meant, love," he added, raising his eyebrows significantly, "although don't for a moment think he would have carried out his threat to withdraw 'High Rise'. That's all it was, a threat. Let's face it, he practically owns the company, why would he commit financial suicide?"

The threat to remove his soap opera was something she had known nothing about. Her curiosity was aroused, but better judgement won the day and she let it pass.

"You tell me!" she replied hotly, "but it certainly

is reassuring to know that you've allowed me to be dragged into this, well aware that his threats were empty ones. It's too late now, I've signed," she flared at him.

He signalled the waiter to bring them some more wine, and for minutes neither of them spoke. The waiter returned and left the opened wine on the table.

"Sophie, don't make life any more difficult for me than it is," he pleaded, filling her glass. "My own job has been on the line since January." He flushed, embarrassed at the necessity to lay open his problems to her.

She waited, still too angry to commit her thoughts to words and well aware that Lionel was leading up to some startling revelation.

"God, there *so much* you don't know," he sighed, "and it's probably better that way – I'm damned if I should have to be the one to enlighten you."

She waited, slowly sipping her wine, fighting the urge to lay into him with questions.

"Do you remember the unsavoury affair over Mitch Peters?" he asked suddenly.

Sophie nodded slightly.

"I really rousted you over the 'phone, but within days I had Markham in *my* office, like a raging bull."

"What?" she gasped.

"Yes! Hot-footed it up from the South West where *he'd* been hibernating – with you!"

"Don't be absurd – I'd only gone to the cottage by chance – I'd never met him before, officially, that is. Besides, he left me there in the cottage two days later – said he was off to Plymouth."

"I didn't know that then, young lady! Of course, I'm somewhat more enlightened now," he confided.

"I don't really believe it – I had no idea that he'd..." she began.

"You'd better believe it love, because he came up to London expressly to sort out a new contract for you – right over my head!"

Sophie was astounded.

"But ... I'd only known him for a couple of days," she defended herself.

"Time had *nothing* to do with it," he replied cryptically, except that for me it did. He warned me that if you didn't stay with the Company, if I didn't sign you a new contract *tout de suite*, my own post could easily be advertised."

"Well, I never ..." she expostulated.

"No, darling, and it's probably just as well that you didn't."

"Then the Sheridan?"

"It would have finished me if you had refused," Lionel breathed heavily.

"I'm so sorry," she sympathised, putting her hand affectionately on his, "why did you never say?"

"Come on, love, it's bad enough I've had to admit it to you even now. I've had a lousy selection of cards in my hand for this game – I've had to play so cautiously. And I had *no* trump card. In this business, if you are slung out, it's permanent."

"Lionel, what can I say?" she pleaded, apologising.

"You've said it, Sophie, believe me," he squeezed her hand gratefully.

"Tell me, if it's not breaching any confidence," she said a moment later, "why was I offered the Hong Kong job – even though it's come to nothing?"

"Well, that was because ... it was more expedient

at the time," he replied.

She knew he was 'hedging'.

"Is there something else I should know?"

He sighed, rubbed his face in his hands as if the whole thing had become too wearisome.

"Just try to think more kindly of Markham, will you?"

"I'll try, but it's difficult to have kind thoughts for a man when he has you manacled to the wall!"

"Promise me, for all our sakes," Lionel begged.

"All right, after all, it's only a matter of weeks, isn't it?" replied Sophie confidently.

"I doubt it, I must warn you of that," Lionel advised.

"After this, Lionel, I *will not* be used as a pawn in the game." She was adamant.

"After this, I doubt if you *will be* a pawn," he announced portentously.

"There is something else you haven't told me, isn't there," she demanded.

"Yes," came the flat response.

"Well?"

"Gregory is singularly purposeful in his intentions."

"Don't I know it?" came the rejoinder.

Lionel bit his lower lip, and made an ostentatious display of clearing imaginary crumbs from the table.

"And he pays well for people to do his talking for him," she added sourly, realising how rude and unkind she was being to Lionel.

"I have warned you, Sophie," was all that Lionel would say, getting up to pay the bill.

Lunch was over.

For the rest of the afternoon she wandered gloomily

around the shops in the City, half afraid to go back to the flat in case *he* telephoned her or called and compromised her in any way. To postpone her return home further, she resolved to stay in town for the evening and visit a theatre. There was a wry significance in the fact that she chose to see 'Fatal Attraction' at the Haymarket. She deliberately picked out the title for absolutely no other reason than it fell in with her own predicament. She later realised than ninety per cent of the performance had passed without her notice because she was too preoccupied with her own thoughts.

When eventually she arrived back at her flat she found a note had been pushed under her door. Her heart missed a beat as she recognised the pronounced Markham writing on the outside and inside in the perfunctory, matter-of-fact, assuming style.

He had called at the flat, early in the evening. She was glad she had pre-empted him and stayed in town. He would 'phone her later that night. Yes, she determined, and I shall not answer the instrument's demanding ring. She purposefully turned the ringing tone to minimum on the telephone, placed a cushion over it and went to bed. If Gregory *did* ring her or not, she had no idea, for there was no chance the ring would have been audible anyway.

She lay awake for a long time, frustrated by her inability to come to any conclusion now about what she wanted from her life. Not for the first time, she attempted to get some order into her thoughts and feelings and try to see her situation from a more objective standpoint, but it was impossible.

Although Lionel had not considered Gregory's actions despicable, Sophie had been on the receiving end and was convinced that his motives were less than honourable.

Gregory had, in her estimation, exerted unpleasant pressure and influence over her life. From the time of her accident she had been made aware of his propensity for ruthlessness. Not least was his determination to wield influence over her job in forcing her to take a contract – but it was what *he* wanted. Worse still, he had manoeuvred his way into her mother's life, acquired her father's notes, bought the family cottage, taken it upon himself to have her installed in a private ward at the hospital.

It was *all* enough to destroy the passion she had felt for Gregory. She felt an intense resentment at the way his will was imposed on others, and had a strong determination to refuse to allow herself to be drawn into any relationship with him. She would contrive to avoid giving him the advantage or opportunity of being alone with her – for she knew to her cost, from past experience, that he could so easily win physical control over her. She had no intention of degrading herself to submit to passion with a man she now clearly despised.

Production for the Sheridan dramas was to begin on the first of June. Sophie felt she had weakened in accepting her contract – as if she had lost in her battle of wits with Lionel and Markham. To justify herself, she argued that a conscience was no bad thing – even though the studio and Markham *had* manipulated her – and in some respects, she sensed a one-upmanship. After all, *they* were responsible for the manipulating, and *she* had been their victim. Let them examine their own consciences, she decided.

One thing was for sure, she wouldn't be able to

avoid him all of the time, but at least in the studios he would have to behave himself and she would contrive never to have any other meeting with him elsewhere.

One thing which Lionel had failed to explain was why Gregory Markham had chosen to be his own producer.

She thought he probably couldn't help himself and had to be at the controls of everything. He manipulated situations to his own end. After all, she reasoned, he had shares in the Company, he was in the position to do just as he pleased. If people didn't like it – they could lump it! He had practically told her as much when they were in Cornwall. She recalled his words:

"My ability to interpret the whims of people assures me of an extremely satisfactory employment until such time as I decide to pull out the plug and say, 'No more of this – your dreary domestic drama has plagued me for long enough'."

It would be quite a change for Sophie since she'd worked for so long now on research. As Production Assistant, she would be involved in providing all the support services for the producer. That would mean she'd have fairly close contact with him, having to attend all the programme planning meetings, making sure that action was taken on all decisions made. During rehearsal, if Markham wanted any changes to the script, she would be responsible for the re-type. She already knew his script so well, but that could not possibly have been the reason he had insisted on having Sophie as the PA.

He had more than once shown that he was physically very much attracted to her, but he surely did not need to go to these lengths to force himself upon her.

At her mother's wedding, he had reinforced his physical desire with the voiced threat, "I *shall* have you, Sophie," which he had murmured with quiet assurance when he had followed her into the Library at Barton Manor.

She had very mixed feelings as she made her way to the first programme planning meeting, making a point of being very early in order not to be compromised by a late arrival. She could position herself where she pleased. At eight-fifteen, she opened the door to 'Planning', intending to set the coffee pot on and organise the room.

She coloured instantly, taken aback to find Gregory Markham already seated, coffee in front of him.

He waved her to help herself and join him at the table.

Obviously, she had no choice in *that*.

He looked up at her only briefly, "I'm glad to see your reputation is correct," he grunted.

"I beg your pardon?" she turned round from the coffee pot.

"They told me you are a stickler for time-keeping and always arrive way ahead of everyone else. Let's hope you can keep it up."

"Is there any reason why I shouldn't?" she asked coldly, annoyed that he should even think her inconsistent.

He raised his head and looked directly at her – there was no warmth in his voice and only a deep, penetrating look in his eyes.

"When I'm paying people to work for me I

expect as much as I give myself – one hundred and ten per cent, Sophie." He dropped his gaze back to what he had been reading.

In some ways, she was pleased by his coolness, feeling less threatened physically, but at the same time she was piqued by his first approach to her.

"You insisted on me," she reminded him, unable to resist scoring, "and if you're not happy with the arrangement I'm sufficiently accommodating to work on something else," she added, sitting at the opposite end of the table deliberately.

"You have very little choice in the matter," he eyed her narrowly.

"No choice, more like it," she added quickly with a trace of petulance in her voice.

"You *do* have a choice, Sophie, working on 'Man of Vision' or not working at all!" he replied peremptorily.

"You call that choice?" she moaned.

His voice had a quiet, threatening tone and as he spoke she watched a pulse jumping at his jawline, "I've no intention of arguing the toss with you, Sophie, when important work's to be done – but I will say this, before the others arrive – I have my reasons for *everything* I do. I make no decision lightly. You will do well to remember that!"

She was stunned. He was so cold, calculating and unemotional. She raised her hand in a mock gesture of salute.

He ignored the action.

"Now, I shall want you here – on my right please, so let's have none of the female devices or histrionics." His voice did not brook disobedience and wordlessly she moved up the table with her coffee and notepad just as two of the production team entered.

No matter how peeved she might have been, no matter how she might be smarting and wish she *could* tell them what to do with the contract, Sophie's more mature voice of reason told her the rent still had to be paid on her flat! She did, admittedly, have a small allowance through a trust established by her father when she was very young – but that scarcely paid her food bill.

For the next three hours, without a break, the outline planning and running order for shooting was sketched. Sophie made copious notes, scarcely lifting her head except to ask for something to be repeated. She afterwards would have admitted she had enjoyed the pressure and the interest of her work. Her mind was totally absorbed and apart from Make-up and Wardrobe, she was the only other female at the meeting.

No-one was sexist in the room. Every person had a job and women were treated with equal merit for the value of the work and their part in it.

Apart from the brief interlude when the make-up lady passed everyone a coffee, Gregory Markham did not relax from his aggressive, workmanlike attitude.

Sheila from Make-up automatically passed him coffee first out of recognition of his position, but he immediately handed it to his right.

"Sophie," he said quietly, "no sugar for you."

Of course, he knew that from Cornwall. She was surprised he had remembered and gave him a half-smile but he ignored it.

More than once his hand brushed her bared forearm as he shifted papers, passed items to colleagues and handed notes to Sophie. He could not have been aware of the devastating effect it had on her equilibrium. A frisson of excitement ran through her and she found it difficult to concentrate.

"Did you get all that, Sophie?" he asked abruptly at one point when she was still tingling with the awareness of his touch.

"Er, yes, sorry – could you just repeat the date for me, Mike?" she asked the outside broadcast cameraman. She hoped she covered up her inattention. At least no-one appeared to notice anything.

"Right, any questions?" Gregory looked around the table finally.

Sophie half felt that no-one dared ask anything. He covered everything. She had to give him that. He knew his business and expected everyone else to know theirs. I suppose you can't fault a man for that, she reflected, admitting that she respected his air of professionalism.

"Okay," he stood up to hurry along the close of the session, "same time tomorrow and we'll go over the scheduling of rehearsals again, as we check out recording and shooting dates." He gathered up all his papers and everyone made to leave the room, Sophie included.

"Sophie," he called her back, "not you – a quick word, please," he requested quietly, not even looking at her.

A quick tremor of fear shot through her. He had been totally business-like throughout and she dreaded, naturally, he might have an ulterior motive in keeping her behind.

"This afternoon, three o'clock, I'd like you with

me when I meet all the cast," he said calmly, leaning against the table.

She drew a quick breath as her eyes could not avoid looking at the taut muscles of his thighs.

"Yes, I had intended to be, it's on my brief of duties. Will the meeting be in here?" she reddened, realising he had seen the direction of her eyes.

"Yes. Now, that may put you under pressure to get the notes out for first thing tomorrow," he pointed out.

"I'll manage ..." she offered.

"No!" his voice was sharp and firm. "I dislike hearing of anyone 'managing'. It's going to mean staying later, of course, but I'll drop you back at your flat."

Shock ran though her. This is just what she had dreaded.

"No – I mean ... I'm sorry, it's not possible for me to remain over this evening," she stumbled, inadequately, hastily trying to piece together a sensible, logical answer, I've an arrangement for this evening ..."

"What arrangement?" he demanded urgently.

"Personal," she said flatly, furious with herself for getting trapped and angry with Gregory for his persistence.

"The work comes first, Sophie," he reminded her.

"I shall work straight through now," she promised, "I would prefer it that way, if you don't mind," Sophie protested. He touched her arm briefly.

"Ring me in my office if there's any problem – I don't like the idea of you working over and having to leave here late," he softened.

"I won't – it will all be ready for you Mr Markham, I promise."

Sophie felt slightly unsteady as she hurried out to the sanctuary of her tiny office. She had roughly three hours to get the bulk of her notes into a top copy. She clenched her teeth and got on with the job to steady her nerves.

At five to three the printer gave up its final sheet and Sophie breathed a huge sigh of relief.

She had gone without lunch, deliberately ignoring the noisy orchestration in her tummy as it tried to remind her that food was expected periodically! Two coffees had had to suffice.

But the work was all completed and an appropriate number of copies prepared for tomorrow's meeting.

It was two minutes to three as she left to join Gregory and she hastily gathered her notebook, making for the Ladies Room en route, feeling very thankful that she had decided to get the work completed. She hated unpunctuality and still smarted from his implied criticism that morning that there might be inconsistencies in her.

Flicking a brush through her hair and taking a quick glance in the mirror, she thought briefly of Mrs Markham and decided she didn't envy her one little bit. Gregory had the knack of making people feel as if they were constantly being pressurised. It was his right, she supposed, owning so much of the company, dominating in every way.

She stepped into the meeting just as the last member of the cast was arriving. Gregory, barely glancing at her, began immediately to introduce himself to the cast. Very commanding, she decided.

No nonsense required from anyone, he emphasised by his direct, authoritative tone.

There were nearly sixty cast members – a huge payroll, she reflected, and this was probably one of the very few times they would all come together.

"In two days, you will all be given the complete schedule," he was saying, "Right, Sophie?" he added, looking at her for confirmation of his statement.

"Er yes, Mr Markham," she flushed awkwardly for he had caught her completely unawares and she had not been expecting to even comment.

In actual fact, Sophie was absorbed in a kind of fantasy as she had been almost mesmerised watching his body movements, lean and lithe as he had shifted from his chair to lean against the window ledge.

The late afternoon sun had lit up the flecks in his dark shock of hair, the white crisp of his shirt dazzling as it stretched against the muscular tautness of his expansive chest. His black trousers hugged his hips so perfectly and she was visualising the moment when he had pressed himself to her so urgently, in her flat, so many weeks ago. Guiltily, she realised she was far too absorbed in Gregory. Oh, why are you someone else's, she ached inside, as the needs of her own body responded to her thoughts.

None of the cast could have had any inkling of her turmoil, but she sensed that Gregory knew the effect he was having on her. His body language was so tantalising and teasing and some of the females in the cast would undoubtedly be straining to test their producer's interest!

Sophie, whilst respecting his professionalism, half-believed it to be a worthy performance within itself, for she had seen Gregory in totally different circumstances – in Cornwall, Gregory the man had a kind of wild recklessness about him, a moody, untameable male. In the room today, he was a man in total control, his true feelings probably cloaked with his armour of effortless authority.

She knew he had an incisive mind and she very much admired the work he had written. As the copies of the script were handed around appropriately, Sophie felt a quick surge of pride. She'd known this work now since those scrappy notes of Gregory's in Cornwall, and she remembered the hours of labouring over that dreadful old typewriter of his at her mother's cottage. The memories flooded in uninhibited until she realised she would never be able to go there again. Gregory had bought the cottage! Involuntarily she stole a quick glance and he was watching her too, but his dark eyes gave little away.

Despite all the undeniable physical cravings he created in her, she despised him for everything he had taken from her. Indirectly, her mother, who had married Gregory's right-hand man, because if he'd never sent Henry to the bungalow in Burnham Beeches, then her mother would still be there – the same as she always had been. On the other hand, she couldn't deny that her mother was now extremely contented for the first time in years, and it was only Sophie who felt left out and on the fringe. She felt even more excluded since her mother had given her father's notes to Gregory, but what had caused her to feel totally excluded was the fact that her mother sold the cottage without even discussing it with her.

She abhorred his attitude over 'Man of Vision', resenting the way that he had blackmailed her into working on it. Paradoxically, Sophie was actually enjoying the contract so far, knowing she was flirting with danger being in such close proximity to such an uncompromising display of masculine magnetism.

The cast were eating out of his hand. There would be no histrionics from this group – he had, above all, their respect, partly because they knew he had also written the drama. He would live every line with them in a way no-one else could, because they were *his* lines, *his* emotions and ideas pouring from the script.

Gregory took time to ensure that the cast were filled in with a potted history of the period, and recommended to all of them that they tackle some of the background reading he handed to them all on a separate sheet.

"It will give you a better sense of the period," he stressed, and there was a teasing gleam in his dark eyes as he glanced at Sophie, adding, "I'm sure Sophie would confirm the need for adequate research in any role."

Aware that she flushed hotly at his attention, she nodded, crying inwardly, don't look at me in that way. It would take so little to surrender to his wild attraction, as one of the cast so thoughtlessly reminded her on the way out.

"Lucky old you, Sophie, you'll be round him every day – isn't he just *so* desirable?"

"I'm afraid I'll be just too busy to notice, Sian," she responded quickly. "I'm paid to work!" Sophie could have added, and he's married, knowing full well that if he weren't, it would have been well-nigh impossible to resist his essentially male virility, for even the most wary female can become reckless around such latent sexuality – especially, she reflected, when hidden needs and hungers drive away something more fundamental than mere caution!

The real problem for Sophie would be his determination to have her anyway, as he had already threatened her on more than one occasion – as if he took his marital responsibilities so lightly. She felt extremely vulnerable.

Sophie made a determined effort to socialise more now that her contract was a strictly studio-based one. It gave her a welcome opportunity to develop friendships with some of the cast and on a number of occasions they went for a meal or a drink after filming. She had almost forgotten what it was like to be part of a team again because, as she reflected, this was her first real contract since the Manchester fiasco with Mitch Peters – who had subsequently been given his marching orders.

The time in Cornwall, the enforced holiday and then the dreadful accident had taken nearly six months out of her life and it needed all her energies to keep her confidence buoyed up at the start.

Gregory kept himself very aloof from her most of the working day. Not that he ignored her, he simply kept his relationship on a strictly working footing. No-one could possibly have suspected that the producer had practically seduced her one evening in her own flat and threatened to have her, in no uncertain terms.

She felt his searching glance on her from time to time, but somehow managed not to allow herself to visibly respond. Sophie had her areas of vulnerability but determined not to surrender to his attraction and so her reactions to Gregory on a daily basis were markedly more restrained and cool than she believed herself capable of.

But at night, alone, in the seclusion of her little flat, she drowned herself in anguish over her unfulfilled needs, realising what a cleft stick situation she was in.

Sophie wanted him, and each day she wanted him even more. She couldn't have him, not morally or legally anyway, so it was a case of self-denial. On the other hand, she couldn't and wouldn't countenance anyone else. She was doing little enough about filling in the void in her life. It seemed impossible to think that there *could* be a man who stirred her in the way that Gregory did.

Each night then became a torment to her and she began to dread being in the flat. She usually unplugged her telephone to avoid his calls – whether they came or not she never knew. She was afraid to even let a chink of the possibility of him creep into her life. The nights she went out filled huge gaps in for her and she was more than glad of the company of some of the cast.

Weeks were passing rapidly, and instead of getting easier for her to be around Gregory, it was causing her more strain than she knew possible. It should have been easier, because *he* made no demands on her, no outward show of his earlier threat. Gregory kept himself remarkably in check to the point where she might even have imagined what he had said to her in the Library at her mother's wedding.

Then, after a couple of months, over the coffee break one morning, he moved towards her with a lazy grace he possessed and asked her if she was enjoying the work.

Admitting that she had found it absorbing, he reminded her with almost savage amusement of her early resistance to the contract.

"You see," he murmured quietly, dropping his voice, "I know just what's right for you, Sophie."

The male scent of him close to her was like an aphrodisiac, and her heart beat heavily in her ears as he added,

"Nevertheless, the day of recompense is very close."

Sophie flinched as though she had been hit. So, he *had* planned everything and it was not mere chance he might have forgotten his early threats.

There was something deep and uncompromising in his voice and she wanted to rebel against his fundamental masculine arrogance. Aware that other eyes in the room were on them, Sophie tried to give no hint of her feelings in her voice, although the colour ran high along her cheekbone and she felt the dryness in her throat as she murmured deliberately evasively,

"So, I will get Hong Kong after all?"

There was a subtle shift in his expression.

"One way or another, if that's what you'd really like?" His eyes were enigmatic, "I told you, everything is just a matter of time."

"Why was the programme delayed?" she asked pointedly.

"It wasn't – it was cancelled!" he lifted mocking brows.

"Then how ... I mean, if it's cancelled ...? She asked, ruefully.

"Hong Kong has been well over-done in my view, and we ... the Board, that is ... came to the conclusion that it wasn't financially viable to do what in real terms was a repeat showing of what competitors had already embarked on. We were too late! We literally *were* on a slow boat to China!" he smiled wickedly as she showed her own amusement. He was quick-witted and she enjoyed that kind of repartee. He moved away from her before anything more could be said.

Sophie felt distinctly cheated, though. Hong Kong had been the dangled carrot and so after this 'Man of Vision' she had no idea *what* was in store for her. Attempts to meet up with Lionel were abortive because all day the pressure was intense. Studio time was costly as Gregory constantly reminded her and the actors and the camera crew. The schedule to finish on time was a tight one. Lionel tended to work strictly office hours and often by the time filming was done he had already left.

Sophie left Lionel a note at the beginning of August asking if he could see her, but a week had elapsed and she had had no response.

The filming was almost over and she had no idea that Friday evening as she drove out to her mother's bungalow what she would be working on in a week's time. Much of her task had been completed under Gregory's area of producer, but there were still a few days left in the control room with the production director and she might still be required for assisting with information for the editing unit.

The time had run away surprisingly quickly. Gregory had shown little sign, as the production was being filmed, of his approval or disapproval. Sometimes she felt the cast would have appreciated an encouraging word, a compliment or two to stimulate them even more. But that did not appear to be Gregory's line. In some respects, she was pleased, because at least he never went 'over the top', gushing the with 'darlings', 'my loves' and 'super' clichés which some producers were prone to!

One or two of the ladies in the cast had fluttered the eyelashes and gave him many a provocative smile, but they never achieved their aim. At least, Sophie wasn't aware of it, if they did. Perhaps his cool persona in front of everyone was an act and he was enjoying himself immensely after hours before going home to Barton Manor! Sophie had no real way of knowing, since he wore control like a cloak. It still nagged at her, though, that because of her own moral code and refusal to compromise her independence, she couldn't enjoy his sensuality while others of lesser integrity may be having a wonderful time.

The idea of imposing herself for a weekend on her mother and Henry was not very satisfactory, but Sophie preferred the option to staying alone in London.

There was so little to do, living in this state of limbo. There was no-one to share her life with and at the same time she had no real inclination to pursue any meaningful social activity. She wondered how long it would be before she could eradicate the longings for Gregory Markham.

Perhaps, she thought, Duncan had done the right thing after all in leaving for Kenya so that he might expunge the memories of his unhappy and unsatisfactory marriage with Vanessa.

It reminded her that Duncan's solitary letter had not been replied to yet. It had come a couple of weeks previously, and much to her chagrin, showed no sign of his wanting her to join him after all. It was a strange letter – just three sides of detail on the quarters he was in, the lack of funding but the freedom to enjoy his job at last. It seemed, after all, that her suggestion to him that he would soon forget about her was right, unless it was just that he was totally preoccupied with his new job.

Drawing up on the front at the bungalow, for the first time in months, Sophie experienced, once again, that peculiar sense of being something of an intruder into her mother's life.

# CHAPTER 10

The following Friday evening, as she was leaving the studio, Gregory stepped in front of her, took her by the arm and, despite her loud protestations, steered her to his car and commanded her to get inside.

It had all happened so unexpectedly and, completely taken aback, she found herself complying with his order. Without further comment, he drove out of the studio car park and took the West road out of town.

"Perhaps you'd explain the kidnap?"
He did not reply.

"Gregory, where are you taking me?" she shrieked.

"Wait and see!" he ordered without looking at her, "and don't shriek – it's unbecoming."

"Really, this is just too much … I have … I'm supposed to be going out this evening," she told a white lie.

"I don't believe you," Gregory replied calmly.

"How would *you* know?"

"You've hardly been anywhere in weeks, you've had no visitors, and what's more, you've stopped answering your telephone in the evenings."

It was true. She had guessed he might telephone and deliberately unplugged it or never answered it. It had rung nearly every evening. She knew it couldn't have been her mother, who was away in Australia with Henry until very recently. Her old aunt never contacted her, and such friends as she had were at work and could have seen her during the course of the working day. One possibility was that Duncan could have been trying to contact her, but from the tone of that one isolated letter, and the comments made, it was highly unlikely.

Three days after she had received Duncan's letter, Sophie had had an unexpected visitor on the Saturday afternoon. Vanessa, Duncan's ex-wife, had called at the flat to see Duncan. How she had managed to obtain the address, Sophie never thought to ask.

"Kenya?" Vanessa had gasped, "What on earth did you let him go there for?" she blamed Sophie.

"I'm not his keeper, he only lodged here when you'd finished with him," she replied acidly, refusing to let Vanessa across the doorstep into her flat.

Vanessa's eyes were calculating and cold as she ran them over Sophie's figure, working herself into a response.

"You appear to be misinformed, Miss er … I didn't catch your name," she said, a derisive smile creased her mouth.

"I didn't give you my name," came the reproof.
Vanessa reminded Sophie of Mrs Markham, only a considerably younger version. Her dress was immaculate and expensive, and despite Sophie's willingness to concede her attractive, Vanessa exuded wealth and affluence.

Duncan had said so little of her really. There had been allusions to her character, but they had agreed not to spoil their conversations with remembrances of displeasure.

Sophie did not like her and not for the absent Duncan's sake, felt a hostility rising in her over Vanessa's insinuation that Sophie had been her ex-husband's mistress.

"I think you had better leave," she had replied sourly.

"He's getting off rather lightly, I'd say," Vanessa flung over her shoulder, as she went down the stairs, "he's had plenty of money out of Daddy, too – we're buying him out alright, and all the time he's been shacked up with you!"

Sophie flushed hotly at the accusation and slammed the door, but the heated words had not gone unheard.

Vanessa had been the only visitor to the flat since Duncan had left.

All that flashed through her mind as Gregory drove out of London. He must have been spying on her or was simply making a calculated guess.

"Have you monitored *all* my movements?" she asked tartly. She looked at him closely, but his face gave nothing away.

He stared implacably ahead as he turned the car onto the motorway.

"The M3! For heaven's sake, Gregory, where are we going?"

"I told you to wait and see."

For weeks she had lived in a state of relative calm with no upheaval to her emotions, just a steady day-to-day management of her affairs which had given an equable phase to her temper. At seventy miles an hour on the motorway, it was hardly the time to flare up and cause a scene, besides, Gregory had no intention of satisfying her curiosity.

With incredible difficulty she contained her anger, fuming inwardly, unwilling now to give him the gratification of knowing how outraged she really was.

"Suit yourself," she shrugged and shifting in the seat to be as far from him as possible, looked from the window on the passenger side.

"I'm glad you see it my way," he answered smugly, "now perhaps you'll tell me why you've refused to answer the telephone for weeks?"

"Am I under some obligation?" she hedged.

"You knew I'd be trying to contact you – why were you so reluctant to talk to me?" he persisted.

"If you wanted to speak to me you could have done so at the studio any day in the last two months," Sophie's voice was matter of fact.

"I don't mix business with pleasure, Sophie."

"Neither do I, Sir Gregory," she said acidly.

He turned off at Junction 3 and took the A322 South.

"Just *where* are you taking me?" she demanded.

"Ah, you're probably not familiar with this route – rather circuitous, I'm afraid, but at this time of the evening the best route to Barton Manor."

She was determined to appear unperturbed at his revelation. His voice softened. "Why didn't you answer my calls?"

"I've been out most evenings," she lied.

"That is absolutely untrue – you've had *one* visitor, you've been late home five or six nights, every Saturday you've shopped early and hardly surfaced even on Sundays – except twice when you were out all day. You spent last weekend at your mother's." He reeled off her movements automatically.

"I don't believe it!" she was stupefied. "Where did you place the hidden camera?"

"There's no camera, I just happen to have good contacts," came the smug reply.

"I think it's despicable to have someone monitored in that way – it's a total invasion of my privacy, an insidious form of spying."

"Well said! But it was a necessary expedient in my case and not quite as insidious as you think. Have you ever read the small print in the lease of your flat?" She dug her hands aggressively into her jacket pocket to hide the white knuckles of anger.

"I'm sure you'll tell me," she tried to sound unruffled.

"I'm afraid the Spender Trust are your ultimate landlord."

She laughed in disbelief and shook her head.

"Tell me, did you buy up the whole block when you knew I lived there? Is it some sort of take-over bid to stop the Rayne family having a place to call home?" she asked with more than a trace of sarcasm in her voice.

He smiled and hesitated before replying.

"Actually, I own the whole street and others, but it's land that's been in my family for generations – but the Spender Trust provides me with no fiscal rewards – my father before me converted all income to provide funds for various charitable needs, not the least being the homeless – which is why 'High Rise' means so much to me, although I don't expect you to see that right away. No, the land and property will always remain the capital asset of the Spender Trust, but the monies go to the needy. I prefer it that way too – it stops the Inland Revenue getting their claws into it as well! The fact that you were my tenant is merely an amusing coincidence."

"Who did you bribe to shadow me?"

He laughed.

"Oh, Sophie, I didn't have you shadowed. I simply asked Mrs Benson in the flat opposite to keep an eye on you – she's been a tenant for years – and it was only meant in that vein – just to make sure you were alright."

"I don't even know the woman, apart from the polite 'good morning'," Sophie said, "how on earth could *she* keep an eye on me? Besides, I'm perfectly capable of looking after myself."

"I daresay, but I do like to protect my interests. The fact that she could give me a 'blow by blow' account of your movements when I called to see her this morning only served to renew my confidence in Mrs Benson. And as to your visitor – when she described her and gave a verbatim report of the doorstep conversation, because you obviously refused to let her in, I knew Vanessa had finally found Duncan out!"

Her angry surprise could not be contained.

"With friends like you, who needs enemies?"

For miles as he had sped confidently along roads she never even recognised, the verbal wrangling had continued. They had passed through Shalford, Wonersh and Cranleigh and she realised they must be very close to the Manor. He took a sharp turn left and swung the car through the gates and up the drive with a masterful ease. As he pulled to a halt he leaned towards her and said calmly,

"Vanessa Armstrong is my cousin!"

"We'll eat in the Library, Mrs Randolph," he had

instructed a small, diminutive, grey-haired lady who had appeared as they entered the house.

"I thought you might, Sir, I have already laid up in the Library ready for you," she quickly responded, "and I can serve just whenever you're ready, Sir."

"Ah, good. There'll be just the two of us," he reminded her as he led Sophie into the Library.

"Of course, Sir," she replied dutifully, leaving them alone together.

"I would have preferred to have had notice of your intention to drag me all this way to eat," Sophie grumbled, painfully conscious of her 'tired' appearance after a day at the studio.

"Nonsense, if I'd asked, you'd have put up all manner of defences and refused to come. This way, I can be sure I have you to myself for the night and we shall be uninterrupted." He handed her a small suitcase he had brought in from the car.

"You'll find all the necessary items you require in here – I took the liberty of going to your flat first and picking up a few things. I tried to choose something sensible and practical from your wardrobe."

Before she could say a word, he took her elbow and showed her up the wide, sweeping staircase. It occurred to her now why he had arrived late at the studios this morning and wondered, with a peculiar feeling of being a victim, whether he had been watching her flat, waiting for her to leave for work!

"No outbursts of enraged nonsense, now, Sophie, I wanted you to be comfortable. I had a master key to your flat so I used it."

Her cheeks puffed up angrily.

"I'll tell Mrs Randolph to hold dinner for half an hour, while you shower and change."

One of the rooms on the main landing had been prepared for her and clean towels laid out by the shower in the en suite bathroom.

He had obviously gone through her wardrobe carefully, and chosen her crepe de chine suit with a matching white blouse. Even the matching shoes were included in the suitcase. She admired his expertise, but felt violated that he had been into her wardrobe and seen goodness knows what of her personal things.

Sophie felt too angry to eat and played with the food on her plate. Any other occasion and her appetite would have been whetted with the steaming dish of Coq au Vin served with duchesse potatoes and broccoli, but now she felt sick with indignation and could hardly eat a mouthful. She had the sense of being totally intimidated by the generations of Markham Spenders staring coldly across the centuries from the Library walls, but most dominating of all was the present Lord of the Manor, seated across the table from her.

"I'm not sure quite what you aim to achieve by all this, Gregory, but I find your methods offensive. You think money buys you authority over people," she fumed, "Duncan was right when he said that Vanessa's family had so much money it bordered on obscenity."

"I suspected you'd bring Duncan into the conversation sooner or later," he sighed wearily, "still," he continued, "now you have, I'd better get the worst over."

She pushed her plate on one side on one side, got up from the table and walked to the window, ignoring him.

"This Duncan you hold in such esteem is *still* married to my cousin," he said, turning to watch her although her back was to him and he was unable to see the effect of his words on her face.

"I don't believe you," she turned suddenly and held his gaze.

He jumped from his chair, moving panther-like across to her, and grabbed her by the shoulders. She flinched as his strong fingers dug into the flesh through her thin blouse.

Anger flared in him and his voice told of control barely held.

"You'd better believe it, because if he damned well shows up around you again I'll personally see him off," Gregory rejoined harshly.

"I rather got the impression you already had," she replied, a smile of sheer mockery creasing her tense face.

"Oh, I've been in touch with him, make no mistake, but not until I met Vanessa by chance one day. I don't particularly like my cousin, Sophie, but what infuriates me, what I find quite reprehensible, is infidelity. I was quite determined to upbraid your reprobate lover – but I *did* wait until he'd left the country so that he could save face with you. I put certain obstacles in your way to ensure you didn't go with him."

"Quite a family affair!" she replied.

"I have as little as possible to do with that side of the family – I had never even realised that Ginger Jock was married to Vanessa. But if he is not prepared to act according to the rules, then I'm afraid he ought to be brought to order," he insisted emphatically. Furthermore, I was convinced *you* did not know his marriage to Vanessa had not been legally finished."

"And I suppose you feel that you abide by all the rules yourself?"

Mrs Randolph knocked and even before she had entered, he had adroitly moved back away from Sophie.

"Shall I clear away, Sir?" she asked, going straight to the table without even glancing at them.

"Yes, please. Is the small Drawing Room prepared, Mrs Randolph?" he asked.

"Why yes, Sir, just as you asked."

"Thank you, and we won't be wanting anything more this evening," he said, leading Sophie out and along the corridor to the room she had once been in before, when in her wheelchair at her mother's wedding reception at Easter.

The couch was drawn in front of the fire and close at hand was a small Regency table on which were standing two empty glasses and a bottle of wine. His meticulous organisation only served to irritate Sophie all the more instead of being impressed by the faultless arrangements. She was unnaturally aggressive in her response to him.

"Sure you haven't forgotten anything?" she asked with a trace of sarcasm, as he handed he a large glass of wine.

Repressively his mouth tightened as he met her defensive eyes.

"Whatever thoughts you are harbouring about me, and despite any reputation which has floated across your path, I despise infidelity. A promise to me means just that. If Duncan misled you into thinking he was free and encouraged you to join him in Kenya, then someone had to put the situation into perspective."

"And you felt it was up to you to interfere?" she protested with a wry smile.

"I said earlier, I like to protect my interests. Whatever went wrong between Duncan and Vanessa is not my affair, and from what I can gather, neither party was blameless. But they are still man and wife, Sophie. Now that may or may not be news to you and it may not even bother you – but it does me. I find it quite disgusting."

"Well," she gasped angrily, "you're not exactly in a position to play knight errant yourself!"
She saw the muscles in his face tightening as he restrained himself.

"Sophie, believe me, when I mentally scripted this conversation it didn't run like this at all! However, I do have some explaining to do. I don't intend to furnish *you* with all the acrimonious and prurient details of my own marriage breakdown, but I *will* tell you this – Penelope was unfaithful to me. Maybe she had good reason – I am not an easy man to live with – writers aren't. But I never once let her down – mentally, maybe, but physically, never."

"I really don't want to know," she protested.

"I'm telling you," he emphasised, "I *need* you to know. When I discovered my wife's imprudence, I was sickened. I can *never* forgive. That is my weakness. Not even one indiscretion – and believe me, she had entertained more than one lover. Do I make myself quite clear?" He paused, his eyes reluctant to leave her. "If you slept with Duncan ..." his voice tailed off and his eyes implored a response.
She remained silent, still trying to take in all he had

just said.

"Did you?" he asked, dryly in desperation. His level gaze held hers relentlessly but she refused to respond.

He caught aggressively at her thinly-clad shoulders, his lean fingers pressing the bone painfully. His expression said so much as he bent his head and she felt the biting pressure of his mouth on hers. The male scent of him invaded her nostrils and her heart began to beat unevenly. He laced his fingers through her hair and pushed her head back, his lips caressing her neck as he undid the buttons of her blouse and slipped it off her shoulder, revealing the bare flesh. Her blood was on fire in her veins. She had no opportunity to protest. He turned her chin and his mouth found hers with a force that sent tremors all through her slight body. His hand closed possessively over her right breast as a throbbing shook her whole body and her chest heaved with the intensity of every breath she took.

She forced her head away in shock, but his mouth captured hers again and she felt too weak to fight him. In torture or ecstasy she clung to him. His mouth bore on hers, pulsing, and she was scarcely aware of her own fingers, curling through his thick, dark hair and pressing his head urgently closer to her. His hands moved across her chest and slid to her hips, drawing and pulling her fiercely into him.

She responded eagerly, aching as his hand caressed the inside of her thigh as he pushed her skirt carelessly aside and his mouth forced hers to open yet again as his body moved hungrily. He pulled her to the rug, supporting her body as he manoeuvred himself on top of her.

Sophie was lost in an abandonment of ecstasy she never knew existed. Totally unconscious of what she was doing, she moaned his name and flung back her head, her mouth wide open, she had totally lost control of herself. Under the crushing weight of his powerful body, she ached with a longing which he seemed to be deliberately increasing with every movement of his hands. She felt she was in a whirlpool of delight, her whole body moving and throbbing under his touch as she was drawn, faster and faster, sucked into a mindless nowhere of drifting milky clouds, filled only with an intense desire to reach an end.

His voice was thick as he murmured her name, pulling himself unwillingly from her. She was only partly conscious and couldn't move from where he had left her so cruelly wanting. It was moments before he spoke and she heard his rasping breath, watched the strength of his throat, the veins so tense, the twitch of muscle at his temple.

"This is no time or place to consummate a love so earnestly desired. I'm sorry, Sophie, to abuse you in this way."

Tears of despair burned her cheeks, and she bit her lip in an attempt to stop the throbbing pain of anguish and unsatisfied physical craving.

"I'm truly sorry, I ...I completely lost control of myself," he helped her from the rug and sat back with her on the couch.
She was too choked to respond. He turned her averted chin towards him, his eyes appealing.

"Sophie, believe me, I *am* sorry it was a passion of the moment. The thought of Duncan sharing you in any way ... I was overcome."

"Forget it," she declared tightly, with emotion.

"No, never. Look, let's have a sip of wine and let's try and start the conversation on a betting footing. I promise not to touch you."

She took the glass from him and gulped it down unceremoniously. She needed to compose herself and quell the physical craving for him that had scarcely started to subside.

"You must give me credit, Sophie, for being a far better judge of character than you are."

"Hmph!" she snorted ungraciously.

"If ever I thought for one moment that Duncan was right for you, I'd never have persisted in my earnestness to have you. But he *was* wrong for you – that was abundantly clear the night we all met at Chez Solange. You weren't together – there was a chasm between you, intellectually and emotionally. It stood out a mile."

"Don't you think you are presuming too much – people behave differently in company than when alone together," she said.

He pushed the fallen strands of his dark locks from his forehead with a weary sigh.

"No! In our very short acquaintance I worked you out completely and I was sure I was right. You are an instrument, Sophie. In the wrong hands you are tuneless, unharmonious, discordant even. But I know how to play you, to bring out the warmth, the passion, the emotion, the melody of your infinite capacities, the subtleties of your moods and feelings. I understand you. And I wanted you right from the beginning, before I even touched you. You changed my plan for the future so radically by appearing like that in Cornwall. I never anticipated that good fortune would be so ready to fall into my lap. You had all the qualities I knew could satisfy me in a woman. You didn't realise it then how much I wanted you, but I had decided I *would* have you."

"You seem to be very confident, Gregory, she responded, "wouldn't the woman have any say in the matter?"

"I knew you'd want me! You responded to me exactly as if I had written a script. Sharp, fiery, aggressive, warm, submissive and gentle – and you have a brain!"

"Thank you," she replied, sipping wine, "nice to know you noticed."

"I've watched and waited as my own divorce went through, not daring to approach too closely because Penelope was watching *me* like a hawk. When she came to the cottage the whole thing was nearly over." He gave her a helpless glance.

"Yes, I knew she would try to seek me out – but she was always trying to lay some case of infidelity at my door in order to improve her own position. I'm afraid you rode into a hornet's nest. Meeting you in London with Duncan allayed her fears and assured me of a Decree Absolute."

"But what were you doing with her in London, that night, if you were separated?"
He took her hands in his. "Dearest Sophie, life is not black and white – we have children, one is only just sixteen. There is a hellish amount of financial wrangling involved, especially with a woman like Penelope – she's like a bloodsucker! She is always much easier to manipulate when wined and dined in a highly civilised manner. I had moved out of the Manor for a while, because she was becoming

intolerable – telephone calls every day, trying to make me change my mind, threatening me with one thing and another. But it *was* finished. I had too much work to do and too many sorrows to drown. I had to be alone."

It was quite dark now, and in the half light of the fire she studied him closely, trying to recall all that happened back on that day in January.

"When you appeared in my life, quite out of the blue, it threw me, you know!" He moved towards the curtains. "I was trying to wipe my own slate clean – twenty years of it – and with children there were some very tangible pieces of evidence on the slate. You can't just pretend your life hasn't happened. God knows, Sophie, there *were* parts of my life with Penelope that had been good – I can't deny that. But they had all gone. Men go through emotional trauma too, you know. But it was unfair of me to load *all* that onto you. When you arrived, you too had some unpleasant scenes to erase from your life. I couldn't ever love her again, knowing another man had been with her."

She remembered his outbursts the first morning they had met. He had been taking all his frustration and anger out on her – not all the years of the marriage, but the things that had gone wrong. He had gone to the cottage to escape, 'wipe his slate clean', as he'd said himself, and she had inadvertently spoiled his privacy. That had not been the real Gregory then – it was a man expunging his past – trying to make sense of it, to redress the balance of his own imperfections.

"Why didn't you tell me you were halfway through a divorce?" she asked quietly. "In Cornwall, in those few days, you could so easily have told me everything – but you told me *nothing*. We were ... well, I felt very close to you then, you could have told me anything and I'd have accepted whatever you told me."

"Exactly!" he said. "What would you have seriously thought then? Too many married men can use that old excuse."

"But it wasn't an excuse – not if it was really happening," she said quickly.

"Be realistic. With what you'd recently been through and knowing your intelligence, you'd have simply thought I was after your body. Although, God knows, I've wanted that too!" he smiled.

"I have misjudged you in a lot of things – I'm sorry for that, Gregory, but ..."

"No buts – there has been a reason behind all I did to get you, make no mistake. I desperately wanted you, Sophie, I didn't want to see you slip away back in London. You can't imagine how I wanted to skip about with good fortune when I realised you were working for *my* company! How lucky a break can a man have? I could have you eating out of the palm of my hand! Everything was so perfect – your academic background, your job, your father, the cottage, the company, everything ... I know you think ill of me for manipulating things, Sophie, but I saw in an instant that I had a golden opportunity to make everything perfect for you too! I felt I wanted to compensate you for everything that had gone wrong in your life.

"Above all else, I knew I wanted you to work on my Sheridan thing for two reasons! One, you are extremely capable and interested in it – it would ensure the extra research would be thorough, and I sensed what a superb Production Assistant you'd be. Secondly, it would hold you within my reach until June when my divorce would be Absolute."

"Wouldn't it have been simpler to explain things to me?"

"I really wanted to give you a contract to love me – but I was not free and I had to play a waiting game. I had to take on the role of producer in 'Man of Vision'. I didn't want you around any other man."

"But you were going to send me to Hong Kong?"

"To stop you going to Kenya with Duncan. I was intending to be away myself and I told Lionel to send you. I had to make especially sure and the only way was to dangle such a carrot as Hong Kong. I wasn't wrong, was I? Still, that subsequently came to nothing – and that was why I took on the producer role!

"But your attitude all along has been so chauvinistic and at times downright unpleasant. You could have talked to me and sorted this out months ago."

"Like at the cottage? If you knew what it cost me, those two nights. I walked into Penzance!"

"What? Why didn't you take the car?"

"I probably didn't trust myself at the wheel – no, I wasn't drunk, only with need for you. I had to go out and leave you. You didn't deserve then what I might have been unable to stop myself from doing with you. No, the safest way was to burn off my libido!"

"And I thought you were in the Tin Mine Tavern getting drunk!" she laughed.

"I still think you should have talked to me."

"Well, maybe, but what opportunities did we get? After you left the cottage I never saw you alone until the night I came to the flat."

"And the note you sent me from Plymouth! It was so curt, just so formal after the closeness of the two days with you."

"Of course it was – I had to remember Penelope at all times."

"Why didn't you tell me at the flat? I've gone through months of self-questioning, moralistic torture. I've thought you were married and I could never have you!"

"Oh, Sophie," he kissed her lightly on the forehead, "I *had* come to tell you – everything. I was glad the telephone rang, though."

She laughed with relief.

"You were? If only you knew. Duncan was ringing from Aberdeen – or so he told me."

"I was relieved all right! I wanted you, but no – I couldn't seduce you – not then, not even tonight. Even if the 'phone hadn't rung, I'd have come to my senses. I still have that much honour left in me – despite what you thought at the time. God knows, I've come close to seducing you though!"

He slid his arms around her.

"Even now, tonight, I just can't bring myself to – I wouldn't. You know you have a separate room, of course."

"Thank you," she murmured, burying her head in his broad shoulder, "but you really needn't bother now – I'm quite happy to ..."

"No, Sophie," he was firm. "I've waited months for you. A little longer will not hurt. Besides, I want to make love to you the first time, where all this began," he brushed his lips across hers and murmured in her hair.

"The cottage? I ..."

"I know just what you thought, darling, but you were wrong. You've never been married. This is your first and only time – I want to make it perfect for you and you deserve it the way it ought to be – a wedding, a honeymoon and a first night of love to remember for the rest of your life, for nothing will ever be the same again."

"Oh, Gregory," she cried softly, "I hated you over the cottage and all the time ..."

"I know, and you were wrong, but that's understandable – I couldn't tell you then, could I? Anyway, your mother contacted me and told me the Mine Company had been pestering her to sell it. I decided to buy it from her for two reasons. She needed the money and I had some to invest. Secondly, it was to be a wedding present to you – that way it stayed in the family!"

"But you didn't know then that I ..."

"Oh, but I *did*, my darling. I am well aware of my own powers of persuasion."

"Oh, Gregory ..."

"Hush!" he pressed his mouth to hers and she offered no resistance to the warm pulsing flesh.

He stayed briefly, not able to cope with the temptation he held in his arms. Pushing her gently back from him he said,

"A temptress, Mistress Raine, i' faith, but I'll deny myself the treasure store of your body until it's legally mine!"

"Gregory, I love you. I suppose I've known all along, but I've tried so hard to find reasons to hate you," she sighed.

"Wilt thou marry me, wench?" he laughed, "as Sheridan might have said."

"Faith, sir, I have no choice, you may do with me as you will," Sophie responded coyly.

"I certainly will, my love, but I'll wed thee first!" His arms were around her once more and his mouth came down on hers with a hunger that only time could assuage.

THE END

# NOTE FROM THE AUTHOR

I love hearing from readers!

You can contact me on facebook
**www.facebook.com/karen.passey** or by email
**k_passey@outlook.com**

And if you've enjoyed *Contract To Love*, please leave a review, so other readers will know!

Printed in Great Britain
by Amazon